A Recycled Marriage

Rosemary Mairs

LEAF BY LEAF

Published by Leaf by Leaf
an imprint of Cinnamon Press,
Office 49019, PO Box 92, Cardiff, CF11 1NB
www.cinnamonpress.com
The right of Rosemary Mairs to be identified as author of this work has
been asserted by her in accordance with the Copyright, Designs and
Patent Act, 1988. © 2021 Rosemary Mairs.
Print Edition ISBN 978-1-78864-932-2
British Library Cataloguing in Publication Data. A CIP record for this
book can be obtained from the British Library.
Designed and typeset in Adobe Caslon Pro by Cinnamon Press.
Cover design by Adam Craig © Adam Craig
Cinnamon Press is represented by Inpress.
This is a work of fiction. Names, places, events and incidents are either the
products of the author's imagination or used fictitiously. Any resemblance
to actual persons living or dead, or actual events is purely coincidental.

Acknowledgements

I wish to thank the team at Cinnamon, especially Jan Fortune for
her input and enthusiasm, Ann Drysdale for constructive criticism,
Adam Craig for the book cover, and Rowan Fortune for brilliant
editing. Also, I owe deep gratitude to my mother and Joan for their
support and encouragement over the years, and to Clive for his
inspiring feedback.

Acknowledgement is due to the following publications in which
some of these stories first appeared: *Freelance Market News, The
Ground Beneath Her Feet, Feeding The Cat, Journey Planner, Momaya
Short Story Review.*

CONTENTS

My Father's Hands   9

What we need is…   16

Lily   33

A Beginner's Guide to Stammering   40

A Recycled Marriage   61

Son   68

To Tell You the Truth   78

Just For A While   92

Red   99

Basket of Eggs   106

Catalina   118

Thud   125

Three Certainties of Love   135

Vermin   147

The Message   156

Lilies   168

Unravelling   175

Crush   194

The Good Neighbour   202

A Recycled Marriage:
& other short stories

For my family

My Father's Hands

I knew something was wrong. I'd known for weeks. Each morning as I came downstairs, I told myself today would be different; everything would be as it was. My mother turned her face when I came into the kitchen, walking to the larder so she could dry her eyes on a corner of her apron. She came out with eggs and bacon, her voice bright; 'Are you not helping with the milking Tommy?' She filled the kettle, passing me on the way to the stove, tousling my hair with her free hand. 'Go on,' she smiled, 'or I'll make you set the table.'

In the byre, there was the usual concentration on my father's face, pressed against a cow's side. I told myself again—today everything would be back to normal. The first squirts of milk pinged into the bucket. When it was full, I gave it to the calves. They slurped, spilling it over the sides of the trough. I turned to my father, but he wasn't milking the next cow. He was standing at the open byre door, looking across the yard towards the fields. He was still, staring ahead, his eyes not moving, as if he saw something besides the red gate and the sheep on the hill. He often did this now, staring, but not seeing, not busy like normal, not coming up behind me, 'Ah Tommy lad, you didn't let them spill it again.'

My mother set our breakfast plates on the kitchen table. 'Still no lambs?'

My father didn't look at her. 'No,' he said slowly. 'None yet.'

I moved food around my plate. She turned to me,

eyes red, redder than before. 'You'll maybe get another orphan this year. There's always at least one…'

My father pushed back his chair, standing, taking down his coat from behind the door, pulling on his boots and going out.

I wasn't allowed to leave the table; not till I'd eaten more breakfast. 'If you see Jimo later,' my mother called after me as I opened the back door, 'ask him to come for his tea. I'm baking, you know how he loves my cakes.'

I had three friends at school; Jimo was her favourite.

'And Tommy…' but the door was already closed.

I had to find my father. He wasn't in the sheds; the tractor was still in the barn. I climbed over a gate, panting as I reached the top of the hill. The Orphan bleated when she saw me, trotting towards me. She was as big as the other sheep now, not puny like when she was born. 'You done well lad,' my father had said when she started drinking from a bottle teat, after sucking milk from my fingers. 'You done well,' he repeated, and I had to bite my lip not to grin.

Where was he? I started to run, down the hill, back over the gate into the yard. He was standing in the byre, where he'd been earlier, his arms folded on the half door. I had almost reached him before he saw me. I waited for him to say what he usually said on Saturday mornings—We need to clear out the top shed, or chop more logs for the fire, or move the cows to another field.

He stared at me, but still didn't speak. I poked a stone with the tip of my boot, flipping it to its green side, then back up again. Then the one beside it…

'I've run out of butter.' My mother walked up the

yard, wiping floury hands on her apron. 'Can you go to the shop for me?'

We made our way down the lane, along the narrow road in the direction of the village. We passed Dan Moore's lane, still in silence. The only noise was the thud of our boots on the road—my two steps for each of his.

'I have to go away.'

I looked at him, but he didn't turn his head.

'I'm joinin up.'

Jimo's father was a soldier. He was in France. He'd killed a hundred Germans, maybe more. It was all we talked about at school. Jimo wanted to be a soldier; he was going to show me his father's gun when he came home.

'You can't.' My voice wouldn't stay steady; I knew he didn't have to go because he was a farmer. 'You have to take care of the sheep. They'll be lambing soon.'

'I can't stay here and do nothin.'

His hand was on my shoulder, but he still wouldn't look at me.

'Dan will do the milkin, see to the ewes.'

He couldn't mean old Dan Moore who lived on the farm next ours.

'I'm countin on you Tommy, to look out for your mother, to help Dan...'

He went silent so I continued, 'Till you come back.'

His hand tightened on my shoulder. 'I'm countin on you Tommy.'

In just a week he was gone. When I got home from school Dan had our cows already in the byre. They were edgy, knowing everything had changed, they didn't like it. It would take time, my mother said, for them to get used to him, but they kept kicking over the bucket. Dan opened and closed his hands, trying to make his bent fingers work better.

They didn't like me either. I tried too hard, Dan said, don't pull like that at the teats. It would come to me, he said, if I didn't try so hard. The cows needed to stay in now; it was too cold for them in the fields. Each morning I fed them hay and cleaned them out, waiting for the rumble of Dan's tractor pulling into the yard.

A letter came; my mother smiled the way she used to. She read it out, stumbling over my father's writing. *Any lambs yet?* she laughed—always her question to him. He was fine, he said, though it was very cold. It was snowing where he was, *drifts as tall as Tommy*.

Dan was late. I started the milking; my full bucket a trophy to show him. But he didn't appear that morning or night. I went to fetch him, but he didn't come back with me. 'How quick do broken arms mend?' I asked my mother. Her expression answered my question.

The lambing shed was full; the pens up one side deeply bedded with straw—ready, waiting. I fell asleep sometimes, leaning against the bales. In my dream the lamb pens were busy like last year—a row of twitching tails, suckling under their mothers.

Something woke me; what was that noise at the other side of the shed? Had I missed the first birth? It sounded again—the soft bleat of a lamb! She had done it on her own. I laughed, running to the house and yelling in the back door to my mother. 'Twins!'

It snowed, showing my footsteps up and down the yard, going into the byre, carrying hay over to the sheep. Each morning they were gone, my boots sinking into another perfect white carpet. I watched my mother watching the sky; if it snowed more the postman wouldn't get up the lane.

The letter—our only letter—was behind the clock on the fireplace. I already knew what it said, but I could hold it, the same way his hands had held it, before carefully folding it, and returning it to its place. We had written back. *Tommy can milk now. He can't wait to show you. Everything here is fine.*

I shovelled my way from the back door, across the yard. The drifts on the lane were the highest, sloping up the hedges either side. Tomorrow—Saturday—I'd get Jimo to help clear a path down. But he wasn't at school. I called by his house on my way home. The blinds were down, the curtains closed. I asked someone, but I already knew the answer—'They got a telegram.'

The log on the fire was damp, smoking instead of burning. I'd forgotten to fill the basket on the hearth. What would we do when the wood outside was all used? My mother held a book, but kept looking up, her eyes drawn to the letter on the mantelpiece, her lips moving silently. Sometimes, she prayed out loud when she forgot I was there.

Still it snowed, crunching under my boots on the icy yard as I opened the door into the lambing shed, turning on the light. Startled eyes turned to me; they never got used to my midnight visit. They were restless, the straw crinkling as they moved away from me. One was lying.

She was in trouble, breathing short and fast. I knelt. Nothing was showing under her tail.

What now?

I had only ever watched over my father's shoulder. The Orphan had been stuck, just its head out. I'd shut my eyes, hearing, but not seeing what was going on. I had to do something, now! The ewe's neck twitched, but she didn't lift her head. What do I do? I rubbed my fists into my eyes—stupid cry baby.

There was movement just behind me—the rustle of straw. I turned, but there was nothing. The sheep were bunched at the other side of the shed, as though something had startled them.

The ewe groaned. I knew what to do. I knelt forward, rolling up my jumper sleeve, easing my hand into her, feeling for a head. The lamb was the wrong way round. I couldn't get hold of the front legs to draw them out. I had to somehow get the lamb's head and legs into the right position. I wouldn't get it out otherwise. The ewe's rapid breaths stilled. I knew, even before seeing her glassy eyes she was dead.

How long before the lamb died inside… seconds, minutes? 'Worth a try, isn't it?' I spoke, not even sure what I meant. I brought my penknife out of my pocket, flicking it open. Steady hands, drawing the blade along the thin skin of the belly. They still looked like my hands, clasping the knife, but they were a man's now—strong and sure—my father's hands, cutting through the layer of fat, then there was movement, kicking under the purple-blue membrane.

'Careful now, Tommy.' My father's voice behind me. 'Just make a small opening, let the head out.'

It was on the straw, bloody and messy. Alive. *Alive!*

My mother was kept busy, nursing the lamb, wrapped up in a blanket in a cardboard box beside the stove. She smiled, pushing a milky finger into the lamb's mouth, her face and voice hopeful. 'He's going to make it.'

She looked up, gazing at me without seeing, thoughts far away. I didn't tell her about what happened. I didn't tell her that my father was with me when the orphan was born. She would know soon enough, when the snow drifts melted on the lane and the telegram came.

What we need is…

When Arnold woke, it took a moment for his eyes to register that he was in his caravan. They must be away for the weekend, that must be it. He turned his head, expecting to see his wife, Noleen, lying beside him on the bed.

He was alone.

The realisation shocked him; he and Noleen hadn't spent a single night apart in their twelve years of marriage. He felt strange and thought it might be panic, until he told himself it wasn't in his nature to overreact. It was more a discomfort that he was alone, an uneasiness, because now he remembered why he was here.

Noleen was ill.

When he thought of it like that, it sounded sudden, that she had suddenly taken ill.

Noleen had been ill a long time, he corrected himself.

He didn't know how long; at the start he'd thought she was just feeling down. Arnold understood that; he often felt low, particularly in the winter months. She needed the spring sunshine, that was what he'd told himself, when he first noticed Noleen's low spirits. She needed to be out gardening in the fresh air, away for weekends to the seaside in the caravan. Then, she would be back to her old self.

But the better weather didn't lift her, and she lost her appetite, picking at her food, and when he commented, she made excuses, saying she needed to lose a few pounds. Arnold had told her she was perfect the way she was, but still she kept leaving most of the food on her plate. Women were obsessed with their figures, that would be the reason, he thought. When Noleen's friends visited, he had noticed they talked about the diets they were on.

That had been the start of her illness—the low spirits, and not eating. She kept telling him she was fine, hiding it from him, but he could see it in her eyes, hear it in her strained voice, and then it progressed to the constant tiredness. She still cooked their meals and looked after their house, but she went to bed each evening after dinner. She would go up the stairs at eight o'clock each night, every night.

But it was the next development that worried Arnold most. She became quieter, until she barely spoke. And she seemed not to hear him anymore, not to understand what he said. Arnold had got a book out of the library on depression, and withdrawal was one of the symptoms listed. That was what Noleen was doing—withdrawing from food, from life, from him.

It was beginning to get Arnold down. He could no longer bear to see her gaunt face at the other side of the kitchen table, to keep trying day after day to coax her to eat; to sit on his own downstairs every evening while she went to bed.

He had never imagined her illness would last this long, that years could pass. The strain of looking after her had become too much, and so last night he had made a decision. He would move into the caravan for a few days. It was parked in the driveway, so he would still be close by if she needed him. The time on her own would help. She wouldn't have to make him meals. She could have a complete rest.

It would do him good too. He had to stay strong, and not let himself become ill, which was something else he had read in the library book, that carers could become depressed as well. What would Noleen do then without him? He *had* to think positively. He *had* to get them through this.

He got up and dressed. He didn't feel hungry, but he made himself eat some of the bread he had brought with him to the caravan last night.

He was a builder, had been all his life, since serving an apprenticeship as a joiner. Most of his work was renovations, and small extensions. It had been a steady income, and when Arnold stepped out of the caravan he stood on the driveway, gazing at his house. He had provided well for Noleen. A detached house with a decent garden—something to be proud of. He looked up at their bedroom window. The curtains were closed.

He walked along the side of the house to the back door. The milkman had been. He carried the bottles inside and put them into the fridge. In the sink were dirty dishes. It wasn't like Noleen not to wash up, but at least she'd had some breakfast. That was a good sign. Arnold rolled up his sleeves, washing the dishes and putting them on the drainer.

After, he opened the door into the hall, standing beside the staircase, listening for any sound upstairs. It was silent. She must have had some breakfast, then gone back to bed.

Arnold went into the kitchen again. He should go to work. He was in the middle of a job, fixing the roof of a terrace and replacing the chimney. But he didn't like to leave Noleen. She might need him. It was important he was here. He looked through the window at the garden. He could cut the lawn, that would pass the time... but the noise of the mower might waken Noleen.

As he gazed out at the garden, he remembered when they'd first married and moved in. After dinner one night they had brought the kitchen chairs out onto the lawn. The evening sun was warm on their faces. 'What we need is a patio,' Noleen had said.

He had never got around to it. He'd always been so busy, working all week, and then they went away at the weekends in the caravan. But they had lived here for twelve years. How could he have never made time in twelve years? Now the green expanse of the lawn accused Arnold—*You should have made Noleen a patio.*

He would do it now. It wasn't too late. Noleen knew how hard he worked, that there was little time for anything else. When she was better, they could have their dinner in the garden on warm evenings

He went outside, getting a spade from the garage.

It was a warm day, and the ground was hard, but he needed only to dig down about a foot, in a big enough square for a table and chairs. He worked quickly, pausing just once to take off his jumper. It crossed his mind that a circular patio might look better, but it would take longer to make, and he was impatient.

By midday he had finished digging. He stood back to survey his handiwork, glancing up at their bedroom window. The curtains were still closed. He told himself not to be disappointed; it was better if Noleen didn't see it yet at this early stage.

He got into his van, making a list in his head of what he needed at the builder's yard—hardcore, paving, sand and cement, and he would call at the garden centre on the way back and buy a table and chairs, so that when Noleen did look through the window she would see he was making a patio. The lovely surprise would make her smile. He missed her smile.

Most of the tables at the garden centre had six chairs set around them, but Arnold bought just two. That was all they would need. Noleen didn't like lots of people around her.

When they were first married, Noleen's friends used to visit often, arriving uninvited at the weekends. They didn't seem to realise Noleen didn't want to see them that much, that she needed time alone with her husband.

He drove home, turning into the driveway, and unloaded the van. He was lifting out the table when a car pulled up behind him. It was Noleen's sister. She walked past him to the house, pushing down the handle of the back door. It was locked. She knocked and waited, before knocking again.

She came back down the driveway to Arnold. 'Where is she?'

Arnold lifted a chair out of the van.

'I want to see her.'

Noleen didn't like anyone to know about her depression.

'She has the flu,' Arnold replied.

'She's in bed?'

'Yes.'

'I want to see her.'

'She's sleeping. I'll tell her you called. She'll give you a ring when she's feeling better.'

She gazed at him, as though she was going to say something else, but then turned on her heel, getting into her car and driving away.

Arnold took the pavers out of the van, carrying them over to the dug-out area, placing a few on the soil to see what they would look like. A movement caught his eye, and he glanced up at the house. Had the bedroom curtain moved? He put up a hand to his face, shielding the sun from his eyes. Noleen must have looked out and seen what he was doing.

He carried the new table and chairs across the lawn, setting them beside the pavers; the next time she looked out she would see them. She would see the dug-out square and the table and chairs on the grass, and a smile would come to her lips.

Arnold checked his watch. It was four o'clock. He needed to push on with the base, so that tomorrow he could put down the pavers.

Wheeling heavy loads of hardcore across the lawn was tiring, and finally he decided to call it a night. He had some bread left in the caravan, and as he ate, thought over his day's work, pleased. By tomorrow evening it would be finished.

He lay on the caravan bed, remembering the weekends he and Noleen had spent away in the caravan. It had been a lovely surprise for Noleen when he'd bought it. He had asked her to close her eyes, taking her outside.

She'd been too overcome to speak, when she saw the caravan parked in the driveway. Arnold knew how pleased she was, that now they could go away every weekend and not have to put up with unwelcome visitors. There was one of her friends in particular Arnold couldn't stand.

She had said to him and Noleen once; 'Well, when am I to be an auntie then? I wish you'd hurry up.'

It was such a vulgar thing to say. It was their private decision not to have children. He and Noleen didn't need anyone else, they knew children would only come between them, and dilute their love.

'Goodnight, Noleen dear.' Arnold spoke the words to the caravan ceiling above the bed. There would be more happy times, more weekends away in the caravan, once Noleen was better. He closed his eyes, picturing the finished patio, with them sitting either side of the table, enjoying their evening meal.

When he awoke the following morning, he was upbeat. Today, he would finish the patio. It would make Noleen better. All she needed was a good rest, and then the lovely surprise waiting for her in the garden.

Arnold unlocked the back door of his house. There were no dirty dishes in the sink this morning, just clean ones on the drainer, and Arnold felt disappointed. He would like to have washed her dishes, like he did yesterday, to have done this small thing for her. But at least she'd had some breakfast. A good sign.

He went outside again; he had to get a move on if the patio was to be finished. He looked up at their bedroom window. The curtains were still closed, blocking the morning sun edging across the garden, blocking out Arnold.

If she would only look out, look down at him. What if he'd left it too late to make the patio? Why had he not done it when she was well? There had never been enough time, he reasoned. A voice inside his head replied, *But it was just a couple of days' work, and you never made time to do it.*

He sat on one of the new chairs. She had never mentioned the patio again, but what if she had often thought about it, hoped he would make it for her. Maybe, this was what had started her depression, that he had been unthoughtful, that she had doubted his love for her.

He looked at the new table beside him, noticing that there was a hole in its centre for a parasol. He should have bought one yesterday; he remembered seeing them at the garden centre. Noleen would expect there to be a parasol over the table. There he was being unthoughtful again.

He hurried over to his van, quickly reversing down the driveway, and driving to the garden centre. He chose the biggest parasol—a bright yellow one. It would be like the sun shining on them on dull days. There was a long queue at the till. Arnold was impatient. Maybe, Noleen would be up; she might have looked through the window and seen the patio table and chairs, and come downstairs.

The queue moved slowly. The woman in front of Arnold had blonde hair—the dyed, cheap-looking type, and silver hoops on her wrist that jangled when she moved her hand. One of her bra straps showed on her shoulder, not covered by her t-shirt.

A slut, thought Arnold.

There was a man with her, and Arnold noticed he was wearing a wedding ring. How could he let his wife be seen in public looking like that? When they got to the till, she turned to her husband. 'Where's the masking tape?'

He walked away to get it. The slut shook her head at the girl behind the till, 'What would you do with them?'

Arnold looked at the parasol in his hands, anywhere but at the woman. He was so lucky to have Noleen. How did men stand women like that? Some of Noleen's friends were that type. Vain, self-interested. They laughed, the same way the slut was laughing now, too loudly, as her husband came back with the tape, putting her arm around his waist. Arnold needed to be back in his garden, away from these people. How could she behave like that in a public place?

He paid for the parasol, hurrying out to his van.

Back at home, he looked up at the bedroom window, but the curtains were still closed. He unfolded the parasol, putting it into the hole in the table. But it wouldn't stay upright.

There had been parasol bases at the garden centre.

He should have bought one! It was the slut's fault. She had distracted him. But he couldn't go back there; he couldn't bear to.

He decided he would make something instead. That would be a greater display of his love for Noleen, that he had made it himself.

He found a large stone behind the garage. He would bore a hole in it, into which the parasol pole would fit under the table. He lifted the stone into the wheelbarrow, and as he wheeled it around the corner of the garage, a car pulled into the driveway, behind his van.

It was Noleen's sister again.

She got out, looking over at him, and then in the direction of the back door, quickly walking towards it. Arnold's gaze followed hers, seeing that he had left the key in the lock in his rush to get to the garden centre. She opened the door, stepping inside. As Arnold came into the house behind, she called over her shoulder, 'I'm seeing her. You can't stop me.'

He grabbed hold of her hair; it was dyed blonde, like the slut's at the garden centre. He hated the feel of it, but he had to stop her. She screamed, trying to get away, but he had her by the shoulders now, pushing her out. She stumbled on the back door step, falling onto the ground. When she stood, small stones stuck to her knees; blood trickling down her shins. He moved towards her, but she was running now, towards her car, reversing down the driveway.

Arnold couldn't think for a moment what he had been doing before being interrupted, and then he remembered the stone in the wheelbarrow for the parasol base. He closed and locked the back door, quietly, so as not to waken Noleen, and went back to work.

He tried to drill a hole in the centre of the stone, but the drill bit kept becoming blunt. His idea wasn't going to work. He would have to go back to the garden centre for a base.

He sat on one of the patio chairs. The parasol was open on the grass behind him. When Noleen looked through the bedroom window she would work it out. She would see what he was doing. All this was for her. Nothing was too good for his Noleen. He glanced up at the window. One of the curtains had been moved, he was sure. It wasn't in the same position as this morning.

His gaze moved to the dug-out area beside him. He should have had the pavers down by now. The parasol had wasted so much time. He got up, grabbing his spade. He would make it into a bigger patio. It was too small; the table and chairs would fill it. Was this all that Noleen meant to him?

He dug, until his palms broke into blisters; he kept digging until he felt better. He would make it into a circular patio. That would look much better. Why had he not thought of it before?

He straightened his back, which was hurting, and realised that he'd shovelled the earth too far behind him, that it had soiled the yellow parasol.

He stared at it, in distress, wondering should he try to clean it, or go back to the garden centre for a new one? The noise of a vehicle turning into the driveway interrupted his thoughts.

It was a police car.

A man and woman in uniform got out. They walked across the garden towards him.

'Arnold Clark?' the policewoman asked.

He nodded.

Why were they here? Arnold tried to think, and then remembered the blonde hair in his hand. Maybe, the slut at the garden centre had made a complaint about him. Why had her hair been in his hand? He couldn't remember.

'What do you want?' said Arnold. 'As you can see, I'm busy.'

The policeman glanced at the parasol. 'Are you making a patio?'

'Yes. It's for my wife. She's always wanted a patio.'

The policeman nodded. 'My wife would be out here, keeping me right.'

'My wife's not like that,' Arnold replied. 'She trusts me. She knows I'll do a good job.'

The policewoman said, 'I haven't had a cup of tea all day. I don't suppose…'

So that was why they were here, for a cup of tea. Arnold felt relieved, no one had complained about him after all.

They followed him over to the house. He unlocked and opened the door. 'Sit down,' he told them, as he filled the kettle.

He opened the fridge.

'That's a lot of milk you've got in there,' the policewoman said.

'My wife's not well,' Arnold replied. 'We haven't been using as much this week.'

'Is she in bed?'

'Yes.' Arnold switched on the kettle, catching a glimpse through the window of the parasol on the lawn. He turned around, 'I haven't time for this. I have to get on with the patio.'

'Okay, no problem,' the policewoman replied. 'Can I use your bathroom before we go?'

Arnold opened the door into the hall, showing her into the downstairs toilet. He waited for her to come out again, but then the policeman said something he couldn't hear, and he had to go back into the kitchen.

'Have you lived here long?' asked the policeman.

'Since we were married…over twelve years,' Arnold replied.

'You'll enjoy your patio. It's great for barbeques.'

'I should have done it years ago. But there was never time.'

'Tell me about it. What do you do for a living?'

'I'm a builder.'

'No excuse then.'

'What do you mean?'

'You'll be handy about the house.'

Arnold gazed around the kitchen. Had he let down Noleen inside the house as well as outside? He remembered the pictures she had wanted put up, that he'd never got around to. He would see to them after he'd finished the patio.

He heard a noise, a footstep on the stairs. Noleen was up! Arnold rushed to the hall door. The policewoman was coming down the stairs. She looked at the policeman, gesturing something with her hands.

'Right then,' said Arnold. 'I don't want to hurry you, but I've work to do.'

What happened next Arnold couldn't remember afterwards. All he knew was that he'd been in the police car, and now he was sitting at a table. A plastic cup of tea was in front of him. The people at the other side of the table said if they could just go over it one more time.

'But I have to go home,' said Arnold. 'My wife isn't well. She needs me.'

'How long has your wife been unwell?'

Noleen didn't like people knowing about her depression, so he said as little as possible. Anyway, it was none of their business. Other people were always interfering in their lives, their marriage. First, Noleen's friends, and then her sister. She had even wanted Noleen to go on holiday, just them. Of course, it was out of the question; he and Noleen hadn't spent a single night apart in their twelve years of marriage.

'Why did you move into the caravan?'

He explained that he needed a break, the strain of looking after his wife had got too much; he needed a break, for a couple of nights. He was outside on the driveway; it wasn't as though he had left her. He was still there for her if she needed him.

'Tell us about the night you moved into the caravan.'

Arnold thought carefully. He tried hard to remember, but it was blurred to him. Then a memory came back, dirty dishes. He was looking at dirty dinner dishes in the kitchen sink. Noleen always washed up before going to bed. It was out of character. He had gone upstairs to make sure that she was okay.

She was lying on top of the bed with her clothes on, gazing at the ceiling.

Her eyes moved, looking at him.

He sat down beside her on the bed. He wouldn't mention the unwashed dishes, not yet. She looked child-like, lying on the bed, even thinner than usual; her clothes were too big, like a child wearing an adult outfit.

'Goodbye,' she said. Her voice was just a whisper.

He must have misheard her. 'Goodnight,' he replied.

He went back downstairs; there was a programme on TV he wanted to see. He was used to seeking company in the television since Noleen had taken ill.

Later, when he went upstairs again, Noleen was still lying fully dressed on the bed, asleep, her nightdress folded on the pillow beside her.

Why had she not got changed? Arnold didn't know what to do. He couldn't undress her. It wouldn't be right. She had undressed in front of him once, humiliating herself and him. It hadn't happened again.

He remembered the dirty dishes in the kitchen sink. 'Wake up.' He shook her arm, but she didn't open her eyes.

He shook her harder. 'Waken up!' She was pretending to be asleep. 'You didn't wash the dishes!'

She knew what would happen next, that he had to punish her. It was the only way for her to learn.

He slapped her face.

She didn't make a sound; she knew he couldn't bear to hear her cry.

Her eyes stayed closed. He grabbed her arm again, trying to haul her up, and something rolled out of her fist. Arnold picked up the bottle from the duvet. Noleen's pills. The bottle was empty.

'You made her take the sleeping pills, didn't you Arnold? You held her mouth and forced her.'

No! He had taken care of her, like always. He had closed the curtains, pulling up the duvet, and tucking it around her.

'Have a good sleep,' he told her.

It was then he had decided to move into the caravan, for a few days, to give them both a break. She'd been taking sleeping pills for years. She was just in a deep sleep, that was all. After a few days rest she would feel much better.

'You were going to bury her in the garden, weren't you Arnold? You wanted to keep her close to you.'

'I have to go now,' Arnold replied. 'I've so much to do. I'm making a patio. My wife isn't well. I have to go home to look after her. I'm making her a patio. She's always wanted a patio.'

Arnold took a sip of his cold tea. Maybe, that was the questions finished now and he could go home, back to his wife. She would be feeling better. She would be wondering where he was.

Maybe, she would be back to her old self.

He pictured Noleen's face, how she used to look when they were first married, before she got ill. He tried to remember things she had said, but couldn't recall anything, even what her voice sounded like.

Then it came back to him. They were in the garden. The evening sun was on her face. She had turned her head towards him, smiling. It seemed now these were the only words she had ever spoken to him.

'What we need is a patio,' Noleen had said.

Lily

22, Upper Station Road
Belfast
BT2 8HD
24/4/2006

Dear Mr and Mrs Carruthers,

    I apologise for intruding in your lives again. I understand, of course, why you haven't responded to my previous requests, and this is the last time I will contact you. I have no right, I know, to ask again, for you to see me. I have tried, through letters, to tell you the things I want to say, but it is not enough for me. I need to see you face to face. This is my final plea for you to meet with me. I will be in Cunningham's Hotel every morning this week.

Yours sincerely,
    Brendan McCoy

This is how he ends all of his letters—*I will be in Cunningham's Hotel every morning this week*. Lily pictures him sitting for countless mornings on one of the leather armchairs circling the coffee tables beside the faded curtains of the hotel's windows. The place has barely changed in all these years. It is the only hotel in their small town. Ray and Lily celebrated their engagement there; they had their wedding reception there; Andrew's christening; his 18th birthday party. And now her son's killer wants to meet there.

This letter, like the others, doesn't match Lily's mental picture of McCoy—the snap shot in her head—the thug in the dock. He had obviously followed advice to get a haircut, wear a suit, be clean shaven. One of his ears had three stud-less holes. By the end of a day in court dark stubble was making his face look dirty. He lifted a ring-heavy hand to his cheek, scratching it. Beads of sweat trickled his brow. He took off his jacket, and rolled up his shirtsleeves—a snake in blue ink uncoiled down his forearm.

The letters are neatly hand-written, with the correct spelling and grammar. Had someone else written them? Each one asks for her and Ray to meet him. Some are longer. Lily expects him to try to justify what he has done, to excuse it. To somehow, now, after 17 years, explain it all. A programme came on TV the other night. Lily reached for the remote to turn it over, but found herself mesmerised, the same way she had been unable to draw her eyes from McCoy during the trial. A Loyalist, who had been convicted of a double murder, was getting out of prison early because of The Good Friday Agreement. The reporter asked if he felt remorse? No. He had been a soldier fighting a war, same as any other soldier. Same as the British soldiers in Iraq.

McCoy however, apparently feels remorse. He needs to tell her and Ray how sorry he is. He doesn't expect them to forgive him. What he did was unforgivable. *I can't justify or excuse what I have done.* Of course, he doesn't expect them to forgive him, but he needs them to know, really needs them to know how sorry he is. Not once in any of his letters does he use the words *Kill*,

Murder or *Andrew*.

What would Ray think of the letters? She has his address, and a phone number. She could contact him. He phones, every so often; at the end of the conversation he always says, if you need me, for anything, ring anytime. She can't, though; she cannot tell him about the letters. They are addressed to him as well; she should…

His way of coping was to blot out the past. Andrew was gone; nothing would bring him back. It didn't mean that they loved him any less, but they had to accept he was gone. They had to somehow move on. 'We can't mourn forever. We *have* to go on living.' He had tried to hold her, but she turned her shoulder. 'Why didn't you just get in the coffin with him?' He was suddenly angry. She had never seen him this angry. He grabbed her arm, shaking her. She was too stunned to respond. His rage quickly wore out and he was crying, holding her too tightly, sobbing.

Lily folds this new letter and puts it back in its envelope, walking through the hall and upstairs. In Andrew's bedroom she opens the window and sits on the bed. On the bedside cabinet is a framed photograph—the only change she has made. She never used to air the room, to preserve the scent of him. When it faded, she could open the wardrobe and the smell filled her—of his clothes and jumble of shoes. On the chest of drawers is the pile of clean washing she put there on the night it happened. She had only set it down when the phone rang below in the hall. Ray got to it just before her. She waited to see if it was someone for her. The colour left her husband's face.

He never regained consciousness. Two days and nights of talking to him, willing, begging him to wake up. Apparently, McCoy just appeared; no one noticed him coming through the pub door. Andrew was at the bar, ordering a drink. The shooting was a retaliation, the IRA claimed, for the Loyalist murder of an innocent Catholic woman.

'Innocent!' Lily had screamed at Ray. '*Our* innocent boy is lying here. How... how can they...'

She pushes herself off the bed, onto her feet. Her ankles get stiff if she sits too long. At the door she glances back, to make sure everything is in order. Ray had wanted to redecorate. 'What about something like that?' He'd pointed to a shade in his booklet from the paint shop. Lily had stayed silent. 'And we'll get some new carpet.' Lily still didn't speak. 'We need to sort out Andrew's things. What we want to keep...'

She closes the door, going downstairs, getting her bag and coat from the kitchen. There's a bus stop at the street corner, but the walk will help her legs, and anyway, she'll have to get the bus back, as her bags of groceries will be too heavy to carry.

Ray used to take her, in the car—their Saturday morning trip into town to buy food. Every Saturday morning since they were married. The week before it happened, Andrew had told them he was moving out of their home. He'd found a flat. He and a mate from work were going to rent it between them. 'More like you and your girlfriend,' Ray had said. Andrew had been staying out all hours; he was evasive about where he'd been, what he'd been doing. 'When are you bringing her home to meet us?' Ray asked, but Andrew laughed it off.

Lily reaches Main Street, but doesn't go into any of the shops, continuing towards the other end of town. The hotel comes into view. *This is my final plea for you to meet with me.* Lily's step falters, but she doesn't stop. She walks up the steps to the hotel door, the same steps she carried Andrew up in his Christening gown, his breath on her cheek; his chubby fingers entangled in her hair.

A couple with suitcases sit at the first table. Lily walks past them, and other people having morning coffee. He's not here. Her sense of disappointment surprises Lily, but it is only momentary, followed by immense relief.

She turns to leave; a man on his own at one of the tables stands. But this isn't…He takes a step towards her, then stops. He puts out a hand, as though to shake hers, but then she realises he's indicating for her to sit at his table.

She needs to take off her coat. Her skin feels hot and clammy. The leather chair creaks under her weight. She is going to faint. She opens her coat buttons, loosening the scarf around her neck.

She makes herself breathe deeply. The light-headedness subsides.

'Would… would you like tea?'

Her head turns in his direction. He attracts the attention of a passing waiter.

She stares at him; she knows she is staring, but can't stop. The waiter takes the order, moving away.

He looks down at the table between them. 'Your husband...' he finally says, glancing up.

She shakes her head, and he turns his face from her, as if to conceal his disappointment.

The waiter returns with a tray. McCoy sits forward, reaching for the teapot. His right sleeve moves up, uncovering the snake's head. It looks ridiculous now—a hard man's tattoo on such a shrunken body.

He gazes at his cup of tea on the table, watching it grow cold. All of the begging to meet her, and now he has nothing to say. Same as her and Ray. Silence after all of the shouting. 'We should have known!' She even heard herself accusing, 'How could *you* not have known?'

'He wasn't in it,' Ray kept insisting. 'No. No. He wasn't.' This was the bearable option—pretending to themselves that Andrew hadn't joined up, that he wasn't in the UVF, a 'legitimate' target for the IRA. What had he done, what acts of terror had he committed that they didn't know about?

'Not one day,' McCoy finally speaks. 'There's not one day I don't think about it.' He glances up at Lily. 'I tried filling my head. Reading and reading. I did a degree when I was inside. I thought if I could keep filling my head, I'd be alright... but you never get away. The nights... I couldn't stick the nights... I,' the tears in his eyes trickle down his face, 'I'm sorry...' His voice breaks. 'So sorry.'

She hadn't been able to forgive Ray, forgive herself. How could their son, their precious Andrew have got involved? How could they not have known?

A couple at the next table glance over at the sound of McCoy's sobbing. They watch him, taking in his grey skin and sunken eyes; the bald pate, mesmerised as people are with the sick, the cancerous.

'I forgive you.'

The words fill the air; the room.

She stands, walking as quickly as she can outside. Her heart is beating so wildly she has to pause, holding onto the railing beside the hotel door. A blue carpet has been rolled down the steps. People gather below; a girl is opening a box of confetti. A limousine pulls up and two newly-weds get out. So young; Andrew's age—then. They pass her, on the steps—exuberant; joyful. The bride smiles at Lily; she is smiling at everyone, the same way Lily did when she walked up these blue-carpeted steps on her wedding day.

Ray.

She hurries on down the steps as quickly as her ankles allow. She has to get home.

6, Glendun Heights,
Ballylee,
BT4 1KS
28/4/2006

My dearest Ray,
I tried to phone you, but somehow it is easier to write…

A Beginner's Guide to Stammering

THE WHITE HORSE

Hi, I'm Sam.

Hi.

I'm.

Sam.

She is on her own now. Hi, I'm Sam. Hi, I'm Sam.

Hi.

I'm.

Sam.

I walk towards her.

'Hi.'

'Hi,' she replies; her lips are shimmering pink, they move into a smile.

'I-I-I-I'm-I'm-I'm…'

The smile falters.

'I'm-I'm-I'm…'

Her hand fiddles with her handbag strap.

'I'm S-s-s-s-s…'

'Simon?'

I shake my head. 'S-s-s-s…'

'I'm Geraldine.'

'S-s-s-s-s…'

'Shaun?'

I shake my head. Stupid. I'm Stupid, I'll say, don't even know my own name. That will make her laugh.

'I'm St-st…'

'Stuart?' she says in a rush.

I go to shake my head, but find myself nodding instead.

Her friends are calling her name; they are putting on their coats. She holds out her hand, 'It was lovely to meet you, Stuart. Hope to see you again.'

ECLIPSE DISTRIBUTION

I've only worked a few months. It's not too bad. It's not; it's really not...

'Hey Sam, you seen m'scanner?'

Davey.

I've seen the photo of his wife he keeps in his wallet. He's not into shower gel and deodorant; if *he* can get someone... but he probably didn't tell his wife he was called Derek at their first meeting.

I shake my head.

He coughs, hacking up phlegm and spitting it onto the warehouse floor. He looks at my full cart. 'Len us yours.'

I shake my head, 'I-I-I-I'm n-n-not f-f-f-fin...'

He makes a grab for the scanner in my hand, but he's too slow, and I duck past him. He calls after me, but the shutter door in front of me is opening, drowning out his words.

A forklift comes in, and the door chunks down again. The driver points at my cart to move it out of his way, and it occurs to me, I don't know why it didn't before. You wouldn't have to speak to anyone if you were a driver.

DEPARTMENT OF SPEECH AND LANGUAGE THERAPY

'It was a S-S-Sunday m-m-morning in l-l-l-late Oc-oc-t-t...'

'You're speaking much too quickly, Sam. Start again, nice and slow.'

'It was a S-Sunday m-morning in l-l-late Oc-oc-tober, about f-f-four months after T-T-Tess Du-Du-Du-Du...'

'Come on Sam, you're making too much of the first syllable. Slide over it. *...urbeyfield.* Say it with me, '*...ess ...urbeyfield.*'

She gazes thoughtfully at me across the table. Behind her on the wall are new pictures for kids. You're meant to grow out of stammering.

'Did you read the leaflet, Sam?'

It's none of her business what I do for a living, but because I've known her since I was five, she thinks we're friends.

When I don't reply she repeats, 'Did you read the Open University leaflet?'

Now is the time to tell her I've decided on long distance lorry driving.

'Lots of people drop... don't continue, at university, Sam. It doesn't mean you can't finish your education. With the Open University you could do it online.'

'L-l-l-long d-d-d-d-d...'

Slide over the first syllable. '*...ong*'

'...ong ...istance.'

She nods, smiling. '*Yes*, long distance learning.'

'…orry …iver.'

She always tells me people will get the meaning of the word without the first syllable, but I've stumped her.

Then, she gets it.

She laughs.

'I-I-I'm s-s-s-serious.'

She rearranges some papers on her desk, before looking at me again. 'You'll need an HGV licence.'

I nod. I know that.

'Have you even got a car driver's licence?'

THE DOLPHIN

'Next!'

'…ish and …ips.'

The woman behind the counter frowns. 'Say again.'

'F-f-f…'

The sound of the shop door opening and closing behind more customers coming in.

'F-f-f-f-f-f…'

'Fish?'

I nod. 'And ch-ch-ch-ch-ch-ch-ch-ch-ch…'

Sniggering behind me.

'Ch-ch-ch-ch-ch,' a boy copies in the queue. *'Shh,'* his mum tells him.

'Chips?' asks the woman behind the counter.

I nod.

'You get a free can with that. Coke or Fanta?'

I shrug. Either.

'Next!'

'Hawaiian burger, no onions and a large chip.'

'Next!'

'F…ish and ch…ips.'

I've never heard anyone speak that slowly. She's tiny, her hair pulled back tightly into a short ponytail.

'What can?'

She breathes in; her entire body expands, then very slowly out. 'C…oke.'

There's a park up the street. The benches are taken. I put my food and can of Fanta on the wall.

'H…i.' She puts her packet of fish and chips on the wall beside mine. 'I'…m Ger…'

Another Geraldine. *It was lovely to meet you, Stuart.*

'…i.'

She waits for me to tell her my name.

I open my Fanta. I hate Fanta.

'…am.'

She frowns, but she should know I mean Sam, fellow stutterer and all, in the same club.

'St…an?' she says, which proves that all stutterers really are thickos, like everyone thinks.

I nod.

'C…ool.' She grins at me; her teeth are crooked. I remember Geraldine's pink glossy lips.

'I ch…anged my n…ame once, be…cause I c…ould nev…er say Ger…i, but then I could…n't say the n…ew n…ame either.' She finds this hilarious, holding onto the wall and roaring with laughter. For such a small person she has a loud laugh. People on the benches look over at us.

'S-s-s-see you.' I grab my chips, and walk away.

DRIVE SAFE SCHOOL OF MOTORING

'At the next junction, Sam, I want you to turn left. You see the sign ahead, what does it mean?'

'R-r-r-r...'

'Sorry to interrupt you, Sam. You close your eyes when you stutter. Were you trying to say *roadworks*?'

I nod.

'I've a brother-in-law who stammers, so I understand, he can't answer direct questions either. That was a good smooth turn, Sam. At the roundabout up ahead take the second exit.

'He went on a course, Tim did, to cure his stammering. *"M...y n...ame is T...im and I'm a b...uilder."* Every time I saw him that's what he said. Dead slow. It cracked me up. Have *you* been on a course?'

Obviously not. I shake my head.

'D-d-d-d...'

The car stops.

'Sorry about that, Sam, I had to use my brake, because you were veering across the white line.'

'D-d-d-d-d...'

He brings a memo pad and pen out of the car pocket in front of him, handing it to me.

Did you say second exit?

'Will I ask Tim for you, about the course? It's just, keeping your eyes open when driving kind of goes without saying, eh Sam?' And he laughs.

Ha Ha.

'Tim lost his sense of humour for a while. He

punched this guy for laughing at him. But at least you can see the funny side. You'll be telling your mates later about me slamming on the brakes while you were st-st-stuttering. So, you're taking the second exit at the roundabout. *Sec...ond* as Tim would say.'

THE WHITE HORSE

'Shut up, Sam.'

They all look at me.

'No, like really, would you ever let us get a word in.' Davey claps me on the back. 'Go on, say something. Anything. No, wait, I'll say it for you. It's my r-r-r-r-round.'

She's sitting with her friends at one of the tables beside the bar. Hi Geraldine.

Hi.

Geraldine.

She doesn't see me; her hair is tucked behind one ear, the earring in it swings as she talks.

I mouth, *I've lost my voice*, to the barman. He puts *The same again* on a tray. In the mirror behind the bar Geraldine walks towards me.

'Hi Stuart.'

'He's lost his voice,' says the barman.

You're at uni? I mouth, after she orders. There are bags piled under the table she was sitting at, with books spilling out of them.

She nods. 'You?'

I hesitate, then nod.

She tucks the hair that has come out from behind

her ear behind it again. Her lips are peach today. She catches me looking at them.

Would you like to have dinner? I mouth, but her head has turned as she pays the barman, and lifts her tray of drinks.

She smiles at me. 'Nice to see you again, Stuart.'

STAMMER MANAGEMENT COURSE

'St...amm...er...ing can...not be cu...red. B...ut it c...an be man...aged. All the instruc...tors h...ave tak...en this c...ourse, just l...ike you are do...ing.'

She sees me before I can duck my head.

'H...i St...an.'

She puts her hands behind her head, tightening her ponytail. 'Do y...ou n...ot re...mem...ber me?'

She takes a huge breath in, then out. 'Ger...i.'

I glance around, I can't get stuck with her, but everyone else is now in pairs. She takes another exaggerated intake of breath, holds it, counts to five on her fingers, then breathes out, one-two-three-four-five, 'M...y n...ame is St...an.'

She points at me.

I breathe in. She counts to five.

'M-m...'

She holds up her hand in a stop sign. 'You did...n't brea...the out.'

Of course I breathed out.

'A...gain.'

47

'Take the next left, Sam.'

'M…y n…ame is S…am, a…nd I'…m…'

'You went on the course, then? Good for you! So go on, I suppose you're going to say you're a student.'

'M…y n…ame is S…am a…nd I'…m a stu…dent.'

'Of what?'

I wonder what Geraldine is studying. 'Eng…lish.'

'I hated English, me. All that Shakespeare and…'

'Thom…as Har…dy.'

'That's the one.'

'T…ess of the bleed…ing D'ur… bi…villes.'

'You took that left too fast, Sam. Just because you've mastered the old st-st-stutter don't be getting cocky. What age are you?'

'N-n-n-n-nineteen.'

'Ha, got you! You see, shouldn't get overconfident. Have you a minder? That's what I call him, the guy from Tim's course who makes him practise. Take the next right, Sam. He gets him to do things, like ask someone the time on the pavement.

'You missed that turn off, Sam. You'll fail if you do that on the test. What did I tell you about being overconfident? S-S-S-Sam was a better driver. What are you doing? I didn't tell you to pull over.'

'D…on't imi…tate m…e!'

'Okay, okay, keep your hair on. I thought you had a sense of humour. It's just a stammer, as I say to Tim.'

THE DOLPHIN

'Next!'

Breathe in one-two-three-four-five, out one-two-three-four-five. 'F...ish an...d ch...ips.' In again for five, out for five 'a...nd a c...oke.'

I punch the air, shouting Yes! Yes! without moving or speaking.

'Next!'

'A chicken burger and a large chip.'

'Next!'

'Just a chip, please.'

I know that voice. She will have heard me say *f...ish an...d ch...ips*, dead slow, like I'm a half-wit.

'Hi Stuart.'

She has a blue biro mark on her cheek, I picture my thumb gently rubbing...

'I'm meant to be writing an essay, but I'm stuck, you know what it's like. What subject are you doing?'

Now's the time to tell her I was doing geography, but I dropped out.

'G-g-g-g...'

'German?'

I wait for her to laugh. She can't seriously think I'm learning another language.

'My friend's doing German. I must ask her if she knows you. What year are you?'

I consider fainting, overcome by the heat of the fryers.

'Sec-sec-sec-sec...'

I try *first year* instead, 'F-f-f...' At the same time

Geraldine says, 'Second year?'

I tilt my head, somewhere between a shake and a nod. 'Y-y-you?'

'Second year Psychology,' replies Geraldine, and it takes a moment to sink in, to realise this is why she talks to me.

She's psychoanalysing the freak.

HIGH STREET

'Ex…cuse me. C…an I a…sk…'

The man in the suit looks at me as if I'm contagious, as if I'll infect him with my speech condition. He hurries on.

Geri gestures at an elderly lady coming towards us.

'Ex …cuse me. C…an I as…k you f…or…'

'I'm sorry, dear, I don't have any change.'

'N…o, th…at wasn'…t wh…at…'

'You can talk to me in a normal voice. I'm not senile you know.'

'He h…as a st…utter,' Geri explains. 'He's prac…tis…ing a brea…thing tech…nique.'

'But he doesn't stutter.' She looks at me as if I'm a fraud. 'It's one of them cons, isn't it? Wilma told me to watch out for people like you.'

I breathe normally. 'M-m-my n-n-name's S-s-s…'

'You're putting it on. Wilma is right, you can't trust no one these days. Shame on you!'

I turn to Geri as the old lady walks away, she glances at her watch, spreading her hands. 'T…en past thr…ee, that's all sh…e had to s…ay!'

ECLIPSE DISTRIBUTION

Davey must have taken my scanner at lunchtime. I can't find him in any of the aisles.

He's leaning against the wall outside, looking at something in his hand, stuffing it in his pocket when he sees me.

'Wh...ere's my sc-sc...anner?'

He turns his face away from me.

'G-G-Give it t-t-to me.'

'I don't,' he grabs me by my t-shirt, forcing me back against the wall, 'have it, all right!'

'L-l-l-eaving you, is she?'

It's meant to be a joke. He'd been looking at his wife's photo. His eyes are red-rimmed, but he wouldn't have been crying, not Davey.

'You ever had a woman S-S-Sam? Huh?' His face is close to mine. 'What's your chat-up line? Huh? H-H-Hello, m-m-my n-n-n-name's S-S-S-Sam. B-B-But you can c-c-call me St-St-Stupid.'

I head butt him. Well, I try, but my forehead collides with his, not his nose.

Now he's on top of me on the ground, squashing my face with his hand.

'Enough?' He takes his hand away and I shove mine into his pocket, bringing out the photo, crumpling it in my fist.

THE WHITE HORSE

'C...oke pl...ease.'

'Ice?'

'Y...es.'

She's at a table in the corner on her own. Hi Geraldine. Can I buy you a drink?

Hi.

Geraldine.

Can.

I...

'H...ey St...an.'

Geri appears beside me.

'Wh...at are y...ou d...oing h...ere?' She looks weird, her skin is orange, and there's blue glitter on her eyelids.

She makes a face at me. 'G...ood to s...ee you t...oo.'

She orders a drink, sips it. 'G...et us a b...ag of cr...isps.'

'G...et th...em your...self.'

She scowls at me. 'You n...eed the prac...tise.'

I sigh, getting the barman's attention.

As he comes over, Geri says in my ear, 'Sw...eet ch...illi ch...ick...en.'

She's a sadist.

I breathe in for five minutes. 'Sw...eet ch-ch-ch...illi...' In the mirror above the bar Geraldine walks towards us. '...chi-chi-chi-chi-chi-chi-chi...' she's standing beside me now '...chi-chi-chi-chi...'

'Chicken?' asks the barman.

'Hi Stuart.'

'Act…ually, it's St…an,' says Geri, glaring at her.

Geraldine's mouth forms the word, *Oh*.

'No sweet chilli chicken left,' says the barman. 'Salt and vinegar, or prawn cocktail?'

I turn to Geri, imploring her to help me out.

'Y…*ou* choo…se.'

'P-p-p-p-p-p-p-p…'

'Prawn cocktail,' Geraldine says for me.

'D…o you n…ot kn…ow,' Geri glares at her again, 'th…at you sh…ould ne…ver fin…ish a w…ord for a stamm…er…er.'

Geraldine looks from Geri to me. 'I'm sorry, I didn't know that.'

'You…'ll kn…ow in fut…ure.'

Geraldine seems about to nod, then changes her mind. 'I didn't hear you tell off the barman for saying *chicken* for Stuart.'

'Y…ou m…ean St…an.'

I open the bag of crisps. The barman glances at Geraldine who is saying, 'I was only trying to help,' then at Geri, 'Wh…at w…ould you kn…ow about it any…way?'

He winks at me.

ECLIPSE DISTRIBUTION

'Look who it is. S-S-Sam the m-m-man… C'mon speak to me… C'mon you can do it, watch my lips, H-h-h-hello D-D-Davey.'

He snatches the scanner from my hand, walking

backwards from me. 'Ask for it back. P-P-Please D-D-Davey g-g-g-give…'

I walk quicker; he does as well… We're almost at the end of the aisle. He holds the scanner out towards me, like bait.

I make a lunge and he stumbles backwards out of the aisle.

'W-w-w-w-w…' *Watch out!* I mouth.

A forklift can't brake quickly; they told us that in health and safety.

The scanner flies out of his hand into the air.

POLICE INTERVIEW ROOM

'He made fun of you, didn't he Sam? C'mon, there's no point denying it, other people heard it. He imitated your speech problem, didn't he? You were both given a warning a few days ago, weren't you Sam, you and David, for fighting? C'mon Sam, there's no point shaking your head, it's here in black and white.

'You snapped, didn't you Sam? We've a witness who saw you charge at him. You could see the forklift, couldn't you Sam? But David couldn't; he had his back to it. You wanted to teach him a lesson for laughing at you. That's what happened, wasn't it Sam?'

DEPARTMENT OF SPEECH AND LANGUAGE THERAPY

'The e-e-e-vent of T-T-T-T-Tess D-D-D-D-D…'
'…*urbeyfield*. Soften the "D" Sam. …*urbeyfield*.'

I close the book.

'Sam?'

I slide the book across the table to her.

'What's wrong?'

'…ad …eek.'

She frowns, before getting it. 'You've had a bad week?'

'Al-ost …ot …rested. …avey in …ospital.'

The frown appears again. Her eyes dart from side to side, as if looking for the missing syllables in the space between us.

I take a notepad out of my pocket.

Almost got arrested. Davey in hospital. He told them it wasn't my fault.

As she finishes reading, I remember that I left something out.

Missed driving test.

Oh Sam, her eyes say.

But I can tell she's pleased that I've missed my test.

No …ong …istance …orry …iving.

THE WHITE HORSE

Coke

'Lost your voice again?' asks the barman.

Geri appears beside me. 'N…o, he…'s a cow…ard.'

She reads what I write.

'Afr…aid n…ot, St…an, I c…an't l…eave you a…lone, you…'re my pro…te…ge, re…mem…ber?'

She follows me over to a table.

'Wh…at's wi…th the no…te b…ook?'

Don't want to sound like you.

'Wh…at happ…ened, some…one laugh at you? *P…oor St…an.*'

Sam.

'You ch…ang…ed y…our n…ame?'

I put someone in hospital.

She's shocked, like I knew she would be.

Broke both his legs.

'W-W-What happ-happ…'

Breathing!

She takes a huge breath in, then out. 'Wh…at happ…ened?'

I'm not safe to be around just now.

She stares at the words.

I start to laugh, I can't help myself, she's so shocked.

'Ha, ha,' she scowls at me, grabbing the notebook so I can't use it. 'Oh, l…ook who it is. This…'ll ch…eer you up.'

Geraldine smiles when she sees me. Great, it's the freak, she'll be thinking, must take mental notes. 'Hi…'

'St…an's ch…anged his n…ame.'

'Oh.'

I wait for Geri to help me out, but she looks away.

'S-s-s-s-s-s-s-s-s…'

I stop, opening my eyes. Geraldine will be thinking the same as me, that this is a re-run of the first time we met.

'St…amm…er…ers c…an nev…er say th…eir own n…ame,' explains Geri.

I breathe in for half an hour. 'S…am.'

'I thought you suited Stuart,' says Geraldine.

Geri rolls her eyes.

'Maybe, that's why Carol never heard of you, because you've changed your name, remember the friend of mine I told you about, who's doing German, like you.'

German? Geri mouths at me.

'I dr...opp...ed out.'

'Oh,' says Geraldine. She'll be mentally scribbling that down—freak can't cope with university.

'What are you doing now?'

I shrug.

'What would you like to do?'

'...ong ...istance ...orry ...iving.'

Geraldine and Geri look at each other for clues, then back at me. The barman comes over, collecting empty glasses.

He winks at me.

THE DOLPHIN

There's a queue all the way to the door. I notice Geri is at the top of it.

'Next!'

She steps forward. 'C-c-can I h-h-have f-f-f...'

The bloke behind her in the queue sniggers.

'F-f-f-f-f-f-f...'

'*F*? Is that new on the menu?' the bloke says loudly. 'Sounds *really* good.'

Laughter in the queue.

'F-f-f-f-f...'

'Fish?' the woman behind the counter asks, and Geri nods.

'And she'll want a ch-ch-ch-chip with that,' the

bloke calls out.

'Do you want chips?' the woman asks, and Geri nods again.

'What can?'

'A co... A co-co-co...'

'Is that new as well? A co-co-co? Must try one of them!'

The whole queue is laughing now.

I walk forward, tapping him on the shoulder.

WARD 6A

'D-D-Did n-n...'

I hold up my hand.

Geri breathes in, then out. 'D...id no...one t...ell you n...ot to p...ick a f-f...ight w...ith someone tw...ice your s...ize?'

There's a snigger from the bed beside mine.

'Sh...ut up Dav...ey.'

Geri looks from me to him.

'Wh...at happ...ened y...ou?' I ask. I hadn't realised her stammer is as bad as mine.

She shrugs, saying some days are like that, picking up the leaflet on the cabinet beside the bed.

'Some...one br...ought it, th...at's all.'

Her face falls. She thinks I mean Geraldine.

She puts the Open University leaflet back on the cabinet.

'I g...ot you gr...apes, but I for...got th...em.'

'S...o I s...ee.'

She tightens her ponytail, glancing at Davey's

58

plastered legs.

'He done this to me,' Davey tells her when he catches her eye. 'You don want nothin to do with him.'

Geri's cheeks turn pink.

'She's m...y m...inder,' I say, and Davey mutters something I don't catch.

Geri turns crimson. 'H-Have t-t-to go.'

'Br...ing me c-c...oke to...morrow,' I call after her, and she glances back, her short ponytail bobbing, trying not to grin.

Davey is sniggering again.

Visiting time is almost over. 'Sh...e's l-l...ate.'

'Who?'

'Y...our w...ife.'

That wipes the smile off his face.

'Hey Sam,' he says after a while. 'D'you think I'm insensitive?'

I would laugh, but it would probably hurt.

The face of the barman at The White Horse comes into my mind. He winks at me. 'Y...ou sh...ould t...ake up st-st...amm...er...ing, Dav...ey, ch-ch...icks really d...ig it.'

'Yeah, right.' He doesn't believe me, but then his brow wrinkles. 'Seriously?'

Somehow, I keep my face straight. 'I kn...ow. It's we...ird.'

He thinks about it. 'But like, *really*?'

As if I've planned it, Geraldine appears at the ward entrance, gleaming hair and lips, her face lighting up when she sees me. I bet she's doing her dissertation on me.

Davey's mouth is open.

'A ch-ch…ick mag…net, *be…lieve* me.'

Davey clears his throat. 'M-M-My n-n-n-name's D-D-Davey,' he tries out as Geraldine floats towards us.

I can't hold it, can't keep in the laughter any longer. Geraldine looks worriedly at me as if she thinks I'm having a fit.

My face is killing me; I have to compose myself.

'Stuart,' says Geraldine, and then she notices the name above my bed, 'I mean Sam,' and this sets me of again. I can't say my name no matter what it is.

A stammerer needs a good sense of humour, I remember someone said that.

I think they might be right.

A Recycled Marriage

Have you ever had a moment of madness? A split-second in which you made a decision, the consequences of which you could only guess, that you hardly dared to think about.

This was mine.

I was going to give Malcolm food poisoning. Oil was heating in my frying pan, in which I would cook the out-of-date sausages I had retrieved from our bin. They were for Malcolm's lunch. Malcolm was my husband of forty-one years, with whom, all things considered, I had been fairly happy. We'd had our highs and lows like everyone—small ups and downs, and a few major ones. We were ordinary people, or rather used to be, before Malcolm retired.

I had heard other women comment on how their husbands changed when they stopped working, how they got obsessions, spending all of their time in the garden shed, or taking up golf and playing every day. But it was different with Malcolm; he had not only changed his life completely, but mine too.

I could pinpoint the day it started. Malcolm was watching TV when I came into the room. He seemed upset. A documentary about polar bears in the Arctic was ending. Malcolm turned to me. 'We are doing this Sylvie. *You and me.*'

He explained how global warming was raising the temperature at the poles, how the bears needed the ice to hunt, that they would starve without it, how they could become extinct.

He wasn't telling me anything I didn't know. The 'green' drive was already in fashion. Malcolm blaming us for damaging the environment was absurd though. Everyone knew that factories were the major cause, emitting their big black clouds into the atmosphere.

It was a shame right enough about the polar bears, I didn't want them to become extinct either, but Malcolm's distress about the programme seemed extreme, and out of character.

Maybe, I could have understood it if Malcolm had been interested in the environment earlier in his life, but I couldn't recall even one conversation in which the ozone layer, or CO_2 emissions was mentioned.

This was all he talked about now. As he tucked into these sizzling sausages it would be the usual lunch-time topic—carbon footprints, or the latest eco-friendly technology. 'Did you know Sylvie…' and he would have more fascinating information for me on how we were destroying the planet, gleaned from his morning session on the computer.

It was through the internet he had transformed our house, finding out about energy efficiency, water recycling and carbon-neutral heating systems. Instead of going on holiday last year we installed a solar panel and wind turbine. Thankfully, they were at the back of the house, out of sight from the road, but even so, the neighbours weren't happy. Unlike Malcolm, still raving about the fantastic south-east wind turning the blades to make his green energy.

I had to go along with him in all changes to our

home, our lifestyle. I could hardly say it out loud, but there were times I would so love to have shouted, 'I don't care about the environment!'

That wouldn't be strictly true though. I did my bit, like other 'normal' people, recycling newspapers, tins, glass bottles and so on. But I was sixty-four; I wanted to enjoy the rest of my time. I wanted to keep having holidays in the sun. Everyone else still went, why not us? Apparently, we couldn't even go on a cruise as ships were as atmosphere polluting as planes.

Malcolm still had his car, but we hardly used it. That was something I was looking forward to when he retired—drives up the coast to the beach. Was I selfish? Maybe, but I didn't care, and it wasn't as though we had a future generation to save the planet for; it wasn't as though we had children.

Anyway, what difference could Malcolm and I, just two people, make? I said this to him during our argument over last year's holiday. You would have thought I'd punched him in the stomach, the look of shock and outrage on his face. I didn't wait for the lecture; I'd heard it before. I spent the weeks we would have been in Spain in the garden. It was wonderful weather. Global warming had advantages after all.

The pan spat spots of burning oil onto my hand. The sausages didn't smell rancid, considering they were six days out-of-date. They were a bad colour when I put them into the pan, but now they were browning, they looked okay; a bit shrivelled, but Malcolm wouldn't notice. He was too excited about tomorrow. It was his big day.

Tomorrow, he was destroying our garden to make a vegetable plot. Firstly, he intended digging out the shrubs and plants, and then he would hire a rotavator to churn up the lawn, ready for a layer of topsoil and manure.

I had tried several angles to talk him out of it. There was the obvious fact that it was our front garden, which everyone saw passing by, which complimented our house, especially in the summer when it was in bloom. His reply to this was that there was nowhere else to put it. Our tiny back garden was full, with the wind turbine, and a large shed to house the carbon-neutral burner of eco-friendly wood pellets and their custom-built hopper.

As for the neighbours and passersby, Malcolm said it would make them realise that they should be growing their own vegetables as well—'We should have done it years ago. All that rubbish we've been eating, when we could have had our own organic produce.'

I couldn't tell him the real reason that I wouldn't let him destroy our garden. We never talked about my first miscarriage, even at the time, more than thirty years ago now, or about the second one. It was 'woman's stuff' in Malcolm's eyes, I knew that. He didn't even grieve. He just wanted me to stop crying, I could tell by the way he avoided me when I got weepy. There would be no children. I knew that instinctively, knew that this would keep happening, that my body would keep rejecting them. We didn't try again.

Back then, I went for a walk, the first I'd taken in months. The rhododendrons and azaleas in the gardens along our road were already in bloom, and I realised I'd been neglecting ours. I bought two roses, one red, the other pink, planting them where I could see them from the house, so that when I opened the curtains in the mornings they were there. They were big glorious bushes now, everyone commented on them, but then they had got so much love and attention.

The sausages were almost cooked. What if they tasted off? Malcolm liked his red meat smothered in tomato sauce, so hopefully that would camouflage it if they did. Anyway, his mind was distracted by his new project; he would rush through his lunch, in a hurry to get back to more important matters.

I tried again last week, another attempt to talk him out of destroying our garden. I had been ironing; he was on the computer. I made coffee, taking him a cup. He kept his eyes on the screen as I explained how much I loved the garden. We had lived here all of our married life; I had planted everything in it, cared for it, watched it grow. It gave me such enjoyment.

'But you'll enjoy growing vegetables just as much as flowers,' he replied. 'I'll need your help with the watering and weeding. Look at this house.' He pointed to the computer screen. 'It's 95% energy efficient. The roof was specially designed to maximise…'

I went back to my ironing, carrying a pile of finished clothes upstairs. I could no longer use the airing cupboard; it was full of germinating seeds. There were rows in trays covering the cupboard shelves. They had shot up—hundreds of tiny green stalks sprouting from the soil—a miniature vegetable garden. I went into the bathroom, lifting a bottle of bleach from below the sink, pouring some into Malcolm's watering can, and topping it up with water.

They were dead by the next morning. I could hear the commotion from the airing cupboard. 'Sylvie!' I went to look, sharing his disappointment, wondering what could have happened? It was such a shame, I consoled, especially since it was too late in the season to start more seeds.

That afternoon he came into the kitchen with a carrier bag, emptying seed packets onto the table. 'I asked the guy at the garden centre. He said we should have just enough time to start another batch.' He whistled, sorting through the packets.

I lifted the sausages out of the pan, slicing rolls to put them in. How sick would they make him? He could have anything from an upset stomach to full-blown food poisoning. I was only buying time; I knew that. He wouldn't be well enough to rip out the garden tomorrow, but what about the next day, the one after that?

The only thing I knew for certain was that I was keeping my garden. Malcolm wanted to save the world. All I wanted was to save my garden. I didn't think it was too much to ask.

If the summers were as hot as predicted from now on, I wouldn't really mind not going on holiday. I could sit in the garden instead, in my favourite spot, with a good book, listening to the hum of the bees in the roses beside me.

I poured tomato sauce thickly down each hot dog,

walking over to the kitchen door, calling in the direction of the computer room, 'Malcolm! Your lunch is ready.'

'Okay,' he called back.

I put his plate on the table, and poured him a glass of milk. If asked, he would say that he knew everything there was to know about me, of course he did, after forty-one years of marriage. He knew with absolute certainty I wouldn't deliberately do him any harm.

What did I not know about him?

He came through the kitchen door, washing his hands at the sink, then sitting at the table.

'If you destroy our garden, I'm going to leave you.'

I was as shocked as him. I didn't realise until I said it that this was what I would do. I could do whatever I liked; I was only sixty-four. I could travel the world. Half of this house was mine; I would have enough money.

His mouth was still open with shock.

'It's up to you,' I told him. 'The garden goes, then so do I.'

He didn't know what to say. He had no idea. I had struck him dumb for the first time in our married life.

I walked across to the kitchen door, pausing to look back at him. He hadn't touched his lunch yet. 'I wouldn't eat those sausages if I were you. I think they're a bit off.'

Son

It was to be the only topic of conversation—the proposed motorway to Belfast cutting through the valley, through the farms. 'There's nae enough fundin. They cannae start wi'out it,' was passed around the market, the sense of relief at this news palpable amongst the farmers.

James Surgeoner stood at the ringside, at the same place he'd watched his cattle being sold and bought new stock for over fifty years. He leaned against the rail; he was getting too old for standing all day.

Store heifers came into the ring; they were fine animals, and James raised his hand to bid. 'Mind not tae get carried away,' Wilbert had said earlier. His older brother had always been known to drive a hard bargain.

'Sold.' The auctioneer's hammer went down. 'Surgeoner.'

James drove home, the trailer swaying behind him with the weight, the movement of the cattle, turning in the lane, the tyres of the old Land Rover bumping over the pot holes. *I must fill those*—knowing even as he thought this that it wouldn't get done. Just like the fences that needed mended, the tin come loose on the barn roof, rusty gates needing a coat of paint.

The cattle, unloaded from the trailer into the field, lowered their heads; it was a long day at the market with nothing to eat. James leaned against the gate, watching them, listening to the tearing of the grass. His body ached with tiredness, and he looked towards the house, hoping the stew was on.

When he opened the back door, Wilbert's head turned as he stood at the range. He hated making the dinner, James knew he did, hated that the vegetables were already chopped, the peeled potatoes in a bowl of water, that his brother had to do this for him.

'How many did ye get?' Wilbert asked, once they were seated at the table.

'Jus the four.' He put his hand in his pocket, brought out the docket, set it on the table, then waited for the reprimand that he'd bought too dear. Seventy-five years old next month, he still couldn't buy the stock he wanted without a telling off.

But Wilbert didn't comment on the high prices, asking instead, 'Any word?' His voice anxious.

James lifted a spoonful of stew, chewing and swallowing. It was the question continually asked, in case someone had got a letter, a vesting order, informing them their land was needed for the new road.

He shook his head. Although, maybe he should tell Wilbert what he'd heard, about the funding. But his hopes would be raised, just as James would like to let his be; he knew better than to trust in gossip at the market.

Wilbert's reaction to the proposed motorway had been a mixture of incredulity and anger. When the surveyors came last summer, going over the farm, making notes, taking measurements, James had kept them away from him, knew that his brother was on the verge of losing his temper. Knew from his eyes, from the emanating tension, that if he lost it with these soft, city types he could do damage, was still capable, even at his age, even with only the one arm.

'Harry were in while ye were gone,' Wilbert said now. 'He says he's sellin up if the road goes through.'

The kitchen window was open behind James, the faint bleat of a ewe up on the hill drifting through it. How would they stand the roar of the motorway? 'Somethin for us tae consider,' James thought out loud.

Wilbert's spoon fell from his hand, clattering onto the table, scattering pieces of meat and potato over it, his face shocked. 'We wonnae be doin that,' he said, as if it was his decision alone.

A knocking on the back door, and James went over, opening it.

The postman held out the letter in his hand. 'I need ye tae sign for it.' He shook his head, 'I'm never gonna be finished this day.'

James rested his arms on the gate; the heifers were lying stretched out, as if sunbathing. One lifted its head, looking in his direction, holding his gaze. *As though sizing me up,* thought James—an old man who had never been tall, and was now slowly shrinking.

'Ye'll get run over lyin there,' he told the heifer, but it was a poor attempt at humour to lift his spirits. It was difficult to believe that the motorway would be this close to the house, passing through the barn, the field in front of him, then across the nine acre. Since the letter came, Wilbert had sat silently in his chair at the range, his eyes vacant, as if unable to take it in. There would be no choice now but to sell.

The heifer got up, coming over to him at the gate,

sniffing at his coat. James shifted his weight, felt the pain shoot through his hip. 'I'm nae longer fit anyway tae do the work.' It was something he couldn't say to Wilbert; it didn't seem right somehow when he'd still all his limbs intact.

Wilbert had been the one more suited to physical farm work, had been able to carry calves across his shoulders, to be fencing at nine o'clock at night, swinging the sledge as if it was the first stroke of the day. James thought of the sons of their neighbours who looked the way Wilbert used to—strong, agile; unstoppable.

James tried to imagine his own son at that age, that maturity—the tiny body just the size, the weight of a bird in his hands. There had been an overwhelming longing in his heart to bury him on the farm, to keep him close. It was such a long time ago, but he remembered distinctly the rawness of his grief. Then, when he'd lost Nora as well a few months later, in a strange way it gave him comfort, knowing that at least her sorrow was ended. They were together, in the same grave at the church, his wife and son, waiting for him.

Later, James sat opposite Wilbert at the range; it had been a tiring day, bringing in the sheep to dose them, everything taking such effort now.

'Ye'll write an tull them…'

They had already been over this. James closed his eyes.

'…beside the bound'ry, that's where it'll be.'

Telling, not asking me, thought James, as Wilbert

seemed to think he could do with the authorities. They should be discussing selling, instead of this nonsense.

He must have dozed off then, because when he opened his eyes, the light coming through the kitchen window had dimmed, and for a moment he was confused, thinking it was Nora sitting in the gloom opposite. She'd have her knitting in her hands…

'James?' Wilbert's voice.

James sighed, closing his eyes again, picturing the speed of the wool twisting over the needles, a smile coming to Nora's lips as she glanced up at him.

'I've somethin… somethin tae tull ye.'

James wished he'd keep quiet, give him peace.

'The midden,' said Wilbert. 'They cannae touch the midden.'

James sighed again, moving position in his chair, trying to get comfortable.

'That's where I put him.'

James's eyes flew open.

'I give him a lift. He were hitchhikin. I give him a lift.'

There was a pause before Wilbert went on, 'Said he were a student. Talked away… on'y then… he pulled a knife on me. He were gonna take the car. It… it were self-defence. I didnae mean tae…'

James reached for the lamp switch. Wilbert blinked at him in the brightness, and then the two brothers gazed at each other.

'Ye're…' James hesitated. 'Ye're tullin me ye…' but he couldn't say the word.

Wilbert nodded. 'Aye.'

But he couldn't mean…
'I kilt him.'

The midden.

James gazed at it, as if seeing it for the first time. As if each year he hadn't piled dung on top, and then taken it away in the spreader every spring to fertilise the fields.

Never knowing what was in the soil beneath.

'Self-defence'—he said the words out loud—Wilbert's words. James had clung to them, like a drowning man to a raft, during his sleepless night. He tried to put himself in his brother's shoes—a stranger hitching a lift, then a knife in your face, a demand to hand over the car. Any man would have done the same, have tried to defend his property. Self-defence—James couldn't blame him for that. He couldn't…but—and this was what had kept him awake all night—not to go to the police, to bury him here, to put him into the ground like a dog.

'Ye'll hae tae move him.'

Wilbert's words. Wilbert's demand this morning.

The steaming stink of the dung, and the buzzing hum of bluebottles swarming over it, was getting to James—someone's son was under this. *Let them find him*—the thought raced through his mind—*Let them find him when they dig the new road, let Wilbert be punished.*

The scrape of fork on plate; chewing and swallowing; the slurp of tea—magnified sounds in the silence between the two brothers.

'Did ye dae it?'

James continued eating, not raising his eyes to meet his brother's.

'I a'ready been punished,' Wilbert went on, as if he knew James's thoughts when standing at the midden earlier.

James raised his eyes, gazed at his brother's limp shirt sleeve. They'd been making hay when it had happened; the baler kept jamming, and Wilbert, impatient as always, hadn't cut the engine before trying to release it.

'God a'ready punished me.'

Defiance—James could hear it in Wilbert's tone, could see it in his eyes, as if losing an arm somehow made up for what he had done.

'It weren't self-defence.'

Wilbert frowned. Must have misheard, James knew he was thinking.

'Ye tried tae touch him, didnae ye?'

James knew what the reaction to these words would be, watched the colour seep up Wilbert's neck and flush over his face, imagined his temper like a wild beast clawing at the bars of its cage.

He had always known about Wilbert, didn't understand how no one else did, knew that it was as much a part of his brother as his temper. Knew that he couldn't always stop himself lashing out, just like when he had a stranger in his car; he thought no one would find out, couldn't stop himself from reaching out to touch him.

Wilbert held his gaze, breathing heavily. 'It *were* self-defence.'

The words spoken with conviction, the denial still in his eyes, but then he looked away, deflated, the fight going out of him. His hand on the table trembled. 'I… I on'y…'

What was his name? James opened his mouth to ask the question, but closed it again, not wanting to hear Wilbert reply that he didn't know the name of the man he had buried under the midden.

James sat in the tractor, but didn't turn the key. If he did, he knew there would be no going back. Or escaping from it. You couldn't sell a farm with a grave on it. And he would always know where that grave was, the exact spot, have to live with the fact that he had helped cover up his brother's crime.

But he didn't have to switch on the ignition, didn't have to move the dung, then start digging with a spade.

Someone's son—the words kept repeating in his head. His family would never know what had happened, never know who was responsible for his death. They deserved to know. Wilbert deserved to have them know. He could get out of the tractor, go inside, dial the number for the police station…

He wasn't fit to do this anyway, to dig by hand. He could go into the house and say so to Wilbert. But even as he thought it, he knew he wouldn't. Why did he keep feeling sorry for him, despite everything? He didn't even like Wilbert, not really.

It was just that there was something pitiable about

Wilbert; James had never got used to seeing him with only the one arm. More than that, to have to live the way he was, to be ashamed of it, to know how people would respond if they found out. James thought of their father, a man of few words, who had let the sting of his belt do his talking; he'd have seen Wilbert dead, James knew he would, rather than accept that a son of his was this way.

When Wilbert was sent home from school for fighting, and later when he'd got into brawls in the village, James had known that this aggression was linked to his frustrated sexuality. Knew as well that his brother was going to have to keep his desires a secret his entire life, and then, with the hitchhiker, he would have misread him, would have mistaken friendliness for something more; James could understand how this had happened, could even sympathise with Wilbert's desperation to be close to someone, just for once.

But there were the words running through his head again that wouldn't go away, *Someone's...*

He gazed through the tractor windscreen at the midden; how could he have buried him here? James thought of his own son, of the garden at the front of the house where he'd wanted to lay him to rest, that Nora used to grow flowers in, but which was wild and overgrown now.

He could put him there! It came to James like a revelation. He could tidy it up, could even mark the grave in some way only he would know.

His head turned towards the garden, blocked from view by the house. Wilbert would be in his chair at the range, waiting for it to be done, expecting it to be done, and James almost changed his mind.

He turned the ignition key.

It wasn't enough, but it was the best he could do, for the parents of the young man who never came home.

To Tell You the Truth

'I'm afraid that's all the information there is.'

My mouth had dropped opened.

'I wish I could help you more, Agnes,' he went on, 'but I know only her name, Mrs Gwendolyn Pearce, and her address.'

Father had sat here, across the desk from his solicitor, making his will, leaving half of his estate to someone I had never heard of.

'What about his savings, you haven't mentioned those?'

'He didn't have any.'

'But he had a savings book, I saw him with it. There *must* be something.'

He shook his head. 'I'm sorry, Agnes.'

I tried to take it in.

'How is your sister?'

For a moment I couldn't reply, the realisation deepening, a weight forming in my chest—there weren't any savings, nothing for Nettie and me to fall back on when the shop was quiet.

'She… she's well, thank you.'

When I returned to the shop, Nettie ran over to me as I came through the door. 'Agne!'

She put her arms around my waist, hugging me too tightly; she was the same height as me, but stronger.

'It's all right, Nettie. I'm back now.'

I turned to our neighbour, 'Thank you so much, Ida.' She looked worn out; I shouldn't have imposed on her at her age, but there was no one else to ask.

She put a hand on my arm. 'Any time, Agnes dear. Bye, bye, Nettie.'

'Fa'her?' Nettie looked around once Ida was gone, as if expecting to see him. 'Fa'her?'

'Father's in Heaven. Remember, I told you? Sleeping in Heaven.' I put my hands together against my cheek.

She did the same.

I gave her a duster. She went over to the shelf of Doulton figurines and lifted one down, holding it close to her eyes, smiling at the painted face.

There was an order to unpack; I tried to concentrate on unwrapping cups and saucers.

Mrs Gwendolyn Pearce.

There were people at the funeral I didn't know, in the china business, whom Father had dealt with over the years. Perhaps, she was there, watching me gaze at my mother's headstone, comforting myself with the thought—*Now they are together again*, as his coffin was lowered into the ground above hers.

How could there not be any savings? They hadn't been spent on the shop, or the rooms above it where we lived. They were the same as in Mother's day. Or on holidays… or a car; Father didn't need one, his days were spent here, except on Fridays when he walked to the bank, attending to any business he had in town. Then, he visited Mother's grave. By the time he came home I would be making supper.

If he had been drinking, I would have smelt it on his breath, and he wouldn't have gambled the money. 'To tell you the truth, Agnes,' he said to me once, 'I don't know how men can waste their money like that at the expense of their families.'

Nettie lifted down another figurine, holding it carefully, the way I had taught her, gently moving the duster over it, as if she was stroking a pet. She loved animals, especially cats, but Father wouldn't let her have one. 'There's enough to do without having an animal around,' he had said, and I knew that he meant Nettie, that she was enough work on her own.

'Me goo girl, Agne!' Nettie held up the figurine for me to see it was clean.

'Careful with it now, remember like I showed you.'

She held it higher, pretending to drop it, a mischievous smile spreading over her face.

The shop bell clanged. Nettie's head went down, busy with her duster again as the customer walked around the shop. If it had been someone Nettie knew she would have gone straight to them, but she didn't trust strangers in the shop, or on the street, keeping her distance from them.

I should learn from her. It seemed to be a mistake to put your faith in anyone. I had been wrong to trust Father to provide for us. Did we not deserve it? I had taken Mother's place, looking after him and Nettie, spending long hours behind this counter.

'Excuse me?'

The customer was standing in front of me.

'How can I help you?'

Her eyes moved over my face. 'Are you… Agnes?'

She was small, tiny in fact, her head the height of my shoulder. She had an open face, a kind face even. If I kept thinking these things then I wouldn't feel threatened because I knew what she was going to say.

'I'm Gwendolyn Pearce.'

She was wearing a good coat—black, with mother-of-pearl buttons; her hair was drawn neatly back in a bun. The white knuckles of her fingers clasped the black leather bag in front of her, holding it tightly; on her ring finger was a gold band.

'I'm so sorry for your loss.' She glanced behind at Nettie, whose head was still down, avoiding eye contact with this stranger. 'This is your sister? This is Nettie?'

When I didn't reply, she continued, 'Arthur... your father, told me all about you both.'

She looked uncomfortable. 'I don't want to interfere in the shop. Arthur was very good to me. I... I don't want to cause any upset,' her words stumbled, 'or change anything. If we could come to an arrangement about the business, if I could have just a small income from it...'

She waited for me to speak. 'And of course you live here. I would never interfere with that.'

'How did you meet him?' My voice sounded surprisingly normal.

The question stalled her for a moment. 'We... first met at the florist's... I was choosing flowers for my husband's grave. I couldn't afford much, just some daises, but I always like to take something. Arthur... your father, was buying flowers for your mother's grave.'

'That was on a Friday?'

'Yes.'

'You met each Friday?'

She hesitated, hearing the accusation in my voice. 'Yes.'

'He was kind to you.'

She smiled, clearly relieved I understood. 'Yes, *very* kind. And he talked so much about you and Nettie.'

'Get out.'

I said it softly; it took a moment for her to realise what I'd said, to look shocked.

'Get out!'

There was the sharp crack of china breaking.

Nettie gave a cry, looking over at me with distress, going down on her knees, staring at the broken pieces on the floor.

Gwendolyn Pearce hurried towards her. 'Watch you don't cut yourself. Let me…'

'Stay away from her!'

Nettie sobbed, her hands covering her face, her body rocking side to side.

I knelt beside her, hugging her to me. 'It's all right, it wasn't your fault.'

The bell clanged of the shop door opening and closing behind Gwendolyn Pearce.

Nettie wouldn't go to bed that night. At midnight I heated her another cup of milk. 'Fa'her?' she kept asking. 'Fa'her?'

'Remember I told you, how he's sleeping in Heaven.'

She clung onto me, still asking for him.

Eventually, she lay down on the bed, her hands together against her cheek. 'Me goo girl, Agne.'

I stroked her hair back from her face. 'Yes, you are a very good girl, *the best*.' Finally, she closed her eyes.

What did Father tell Gwendolyn Pearce about Nettie? I wondered did he tell her that he dropped her when she was a baby. No, he wouldn't have told her that. He wouldn't have said, 'To tell you the truth, it is my fault that Nettie is brain damaged.'

He and Mother let everyone believe that Nettie was born that way, but I was there when it happened. I was four years old; I saw her fall, her head crunching as it hit the tiled floor, covering my ears as my mother screamed.

I never told anyone. Although, I had intended to tell Samuel once we were married. I didn't want there to be secrets between us. 'Remember, Samuel?' I said to Nettie. 'You liked him, didn't you?'

She gave a small snore.

'He liked you too.'

Gwendolyn Pearce returned days later. I wondered what Father had called her: *Dearest Gwendolyn* or *My darling Gwen*. She had on the same expensive coat; he would have paid for it from his savings, *our* savings. They would have held hands as they walked from the dressmaker's. Samuel wouldn't hold my hand in front of Father, or sit too close to me, everything had to be proper.

'Hello, Agnes.' Her voice shook slightly, and she glanced beyond me towards the open doorway into the store. Nettie wasn't in there. I had taken her next door to see Ida's cat, and she wouldn't part from it.

She cleared her throat. 'I don't think I made myself clear before. I just need a *very* small income from the business. You see I don't have enough money to make ends meet. I wouldn't be here otherwise.'

She blinked back tears. 'He was lonely. Arthur was lonely, like me. We found comfort in each other. We were friends, Agnes, nothing more.'

'Why didn't he tell me about you then?'

'He…was going to, but he didn't know if you would understand. He didn't want to upset you.'

I almost laughed. Did he not think giving away half of Nettie and my inheritance would upset me? The realisation struck me—what if she could make us sell the shop to get her share?

'I'm sorry that… I have to come here.' Her eyes filled. She unclasped her handbag, fumbling in it, bringing out a handkerchief.

Father must have loved her, another realisation, why else would he have provided for her in his will; it couldn't have just been friendship on his part. She said he was lonely; of course he was lonely, living all those years without Mother. Memories weren't enough; I knew that. My memory of Samuel was fading, no matter how hard I tried to cling onto it. No matter how much I tried to picture his face, and remember the touch of his fingers on mine. Even his voice was fading, the way he'd say, 'Hello Nettles!' making her giggle, covering her face with her hands so he wouldn't see that she was blushing.

I had to keep our shop, our home, not let it be sold. I tried to make my voice agreeable, 'A small income seems… reasonable.'

Her face broke into a smile. 'Thank you, Agnes. Thank you so much!'

At the shop door, she turned back to look at me, pulling on her gloves, giving me a small wave, a mixture of relief and gratitude. She looked childlike, somehow, despite her coat and shoes, her bag and gloves, because of her height and small frame. Yes, Father must have loved her; he probably felt protective towards her.

I closed my eyes once she had gone. I used to pray that Samuel would come back, that he would realise how much he loved me and appear again one day. But as time passed, and hope changed to despair, I altered my prayer. Instead, I asked God to give me the strength to go on. My prayer was answered, just like it would be again.

The paperwork for the shop was in a bureau upstairs. The drawers were crammed. It had been Mother who had taken care of the accounts; afterwards Father hadn't been as meticulous. His savings book would be here somewhere. He couldn't have spent them all, a lifetime of savings on Gwendolyn Pearce! But it wasn't in any of the drawers; all I found were invoices and receipts, yellowed with age.

At the back of the last drawer was a large blank envelope. My pulse quickened—the book would be in it; there would be savings, something for Nettie and me! It felt as if it contained more than one item. Perhaps, there was cash too! Now the overdue stock bills could be paid—we could have new clothes—afford a pet, a cat for Nettie. It would settle her, take her mind off…

I emptied the contents.

My smile faded. Inside, were smaller envelopes

addressed to Father, that was all. I opened one, my fingers lacklustre, unfolding the letter it contained; my eyes moved down to the signature…

Yours sincerely,
  Samuel Trent.

Then my focus rushed back up to the top:

Dear Arthur,
  Thank you for your reply. I cannot express how sorry I am to hear that Agnes's health is deteriorating. I think of her every day, often wishing we had married, that despite her condition I could have cared for her.
  She is lucky to have a father such as you to look after her. I feel ashamed that I chose not to. It must be very difficult for you having both daughters suffering from this terrible affliction. The thought that Agnes is losing her mental capabilities and will soon become like Nettie is unbearable for me to contemplate, as I trust it is for you…

Gwendolyn Pearce came back at the end of the week. I was pricing tea sets, setting them in matching piles on the counter. She walked towards me, past Nettie, dusting the Toby jugs.

Her eyes were bright, a smile of greeting on her lips.

I shook my head.

The smile faltered.

'The shop doesn't make enough to pay you an income. It will barely keep Nettie and me.'

It took a moment to register, for her face to become crestfallen.

'Father had savings, but he spent them all.' My gaze travelled down her good coat to the expensive leather bag clasped in front of her.

'To tell you the truth,' I went on, and her eyes widened recognising Father's phrase, 'I can scarcely believe it either. I thought he would have wanted to provide for his daughters.'

Her head turned towards Nettie, guilt passing over her face.

The next plate had a dirty mark on it. I went through the door into the store, my hands were shaking as I found a duster, rubbing at the mark.

'Agnes?'

She was at the doorway.

'I'm sorry, but I've no one else to turn to. What am I to do?'

She had no one to turn to? What about me? Father kept me here to look after him. How could he have told such lies to Samuel, while all the time he was...

The plate was already flying through the air towards her before I realised what I'd done. It hit the door frame beside her, smashing loudly on the tiled floor. Nettie cried out at the breaking china.

'Get out!' I screamed.

She came towards me. 'Agnes, please...'

'Get away from me!'

She tried to take hold of my hand, '*Please*, Agnes, you're the only one I can turn to. If I don't pay my rent this week I'll be put out.'

I pushed her hand off mine, seeing Nettie behind her at the store doorway, her face stricken.

'It's all right,' I called to her, but her eyes were transfixed on Gwendolyn Pearce, I could see the horror in them, and I realised what she was thinking—this stranger was going to harm her sister!

She picked up the hammer on the shelf.

'*No!*' but she was already raising it in the air.

There was a crunch, similar to the one Nettie's skull had made those years ago, and Gwendolyn Pearce swayed for a moment, then fell forward. I tried to catch her as she went down, but she slumped through my arms to the floor.

I stood transfixed, the same way Nettie had been a moment ago, looking down at her.

'Agne?'

I raised my eyes.

Nettie was waiting for my response, so she would know how to react.

'I… I'll help… the lady up. You… finish dusting.'

She set the hammer carefully down on the shelf where she had got it, going back into the shop.

I knelt; her head was on her arm; I couldn't see her face.

But then she slowly turned her head, her eyes focusing on mine. She tried to speak, her mouth opening and closing, but no sound.

'Don't try to talk. You're going to be fine.'

Her focus left my face.

'*Gwendolyn?*' I took hold of her hand. 'I'm going for help now. Try to…'

Her eyes stilled, her hand slipping out of mine.

Nettie didn't understand why we couldn't go downstairs.

'The shop's closed today.'

'Fa'her?' She looked around her.

'He's in Heav…' The words choked in my throat.

I had to concentrate on practical things. There was the packing to finish; we could take only one small suitcase I could carry. Once we found Samuel, he would provide everything else we needed. His address was on the letters. We would get a train there. What if he had moved? I closed my eyes. I'd promised myself I would pray only for strength. *Please God, let us find him.*

When I opened my eyes, Nettie wasn't there. She wasn't in the bathroom or the bedrooms. I hurried downstairs. She was at the shop door. Ida was at the other side of the glass, leaning on her stick.

I had to unlock the door.

'Is anything the matter, Agnes?'

'No, we're fine.'

She looked past me into the shop.

'I… I'm stock taking. That's why we're closed.'

Nettie took Ida's hand, leading her through the doorway.

'No, Nettie! Leave Ida alone!'

'What is it, Nettie?' Ida put her face closer to Nettie's, to hear what she was saying.

'Fall… me make her… me help Agne.'

When Ida didn't understand what she was trying to tell her, Nettie became frustrated, trying to show her instead, lifting up her hand above her head, then bringing it quickly down.

Ida looked at me. I shrugged; I didn't know what she meant either.

Nettie pulled Ida by the hand towards the store door. I couldn't stop her, nothing I could say would stop her.

She pushed down the handle.

When the door didn't open, she pushed it down again.

'It's locked Nettie, dear.' Ida drew her hand away from the handle.

I took Ida to one side, explaining, 'She keeps mixing up the stock take.'

'I'm going home now, Nettie. I'll see you later.'

'Kitty,' said Nettie.

'You'll see Ida's cat tomorrow.'

Upstairs again, I put the packed suitcase into the wardrobe so that Nettie wouldn't see it.

'*Kitty.*'

'Tomorrow.' I never used to tell lies.

My gaze moved to the framed photograph of Mother and Father on the sideboard. There had been no room for it in the case…They couldn't help us now anyway.

'*Kitty*, Agne!'

'Tomorrow, Nettie.'

I closed my eyes. Strength, that was all I asked for, the strength to go on.

If Samuel had loved me, the way I loved him, he would have stayed, he would have married me regardless. It wouldn't have mattered what Father said, that he told him I'd become like Nettie, because it didn't alter anything, not if he had really loved me.

I poured milk into a saucepan for Nettie's bedtime drink.

This time tomorrow night: '*To tell you the truth, Samuel, I don't remember what happened. Just that the hammer was in my hand, then she was on the floor... I need you to look after Nettie.*'

He hadn't wanted to look after me.

I struck a match, switching on the cooker ring; the gas hissed.

No one to turn to. Gwendolyn's words.

I watched the flickering flame in my fingers.

'Fa'her? Fa'her?'

I blew out the match, walking over to Nettie, sitting beside her. She turned her head towards the cooker, as if hearing the hiss of the gas.

I put my hands together against my cheek, waiting for Nettie to do the same.

Mother and Father were sleeping. Gwendolyn was sleeping.

I smiled at Nettie. She smiled back.

My arm went around her, and she rested her head on my shoulder.

I put my fingers on her eyes, closing the lids, the same way I had done for Gwendolyn. 'Time to go to sleep.'

'Fa'her...' she mumbled.

I closed my own eyes, telling her for the last time, 'He's sleeping, Nettie. Sleeping in Heaven.'

Just For A While

'This is Cathy,' I'm told. 'I'll be living with her for a while.' That's what they always say, 'Just for a while, Tina.' Cathy takes me outside to her car. She drives and talks about herself, her house. This is what they all do.

Maybe, someday they'll ask about my house. 'It's not a house,' I'll say. 'It's a flat; twelfth floor.' Ma complains when the lift's broke. The stairs make her cough. When he lived with us, Mick said they kept you fit. Didn't make him thin though. He's not like Ma and me. Two stick insects, he called us.

'Here we are then.' Cathy stops the car. There is a gate, grass and flowers, a path; houses joined in a row. Inside, I wait for her to say what they always say—'This is your room, Tina. Make yourself at home.'

She asks, 'Fish fingers okay for tea?' When I make them for Ma and me the oil spits on my hands as I drop them in the pan—two for me, two for Ma. She only takes a bite from one, that's all. Mick finished what she left, shoving it in his big gob.

Cathy walks me to school each day. She knows I can go on the bus, but she needs the exercise. She walks fast, swinging the pink plastic box in her hand. 'Maybe, I could walk myself thin. What do you think?' She walks even faster. 'Come on slow coach, keep up!'

The pink box has my lunch—today it's cheese and tomato sarnies, two jaffa cakes and a banana. Kim Gault watches me pick out the tomato and drop it on the ground. 'See you've got a new mummy.' She holds her coke bottle to her mouth, rolling her head. 'She a wino too?'

Her face hurts my hand. I almost cry out, but Kim is yelling loud enough for us both. 'It's your last warning, next time you'll be expelled,' Cathy says that night. 'Tell me what happened. Why did you do it, Tina?' I think of an answer later, in bed. 'She had it comin.' That's what Mick said. My hand is still sore. I go downstairs. The front and back door are locked. There's no electric fire to check. There's a pan on the cooker, but it's all right cause the switch is off. When I came home from school, I could smell it soon as I opened the door. The pan on the cooker was black; the smoke choked me. Ma's head was on her arm on the table. She wouldn't wake up.

'I couldn't sleep either.' Cathy has come into the kitchen. She opens the fridge. 'Will we have some hot milk?'

She hands me a mug, sitting opposite me at the table. 'When I was about your age, Tina, my parents were in a car accident. I was left on my own, and I went to live with an old lady who was very kind to me, but I hated her. I hated everyone. One night I went outside and pulled all the heads off her flowers. She loved her garden and it made her sad. She said, "I know you're angry because life isn't fair. But did it really make you feel better, taking it out on the flowers?"'

The pink lunch box is always full to the top. I sell the biscuits and chocolate for 20p, 50p; buy or else. Tonight, we're going to McDonalds, as a treat. Cathy really needs one. That's what her new diet book says—'Give yourself a small treat occasionally.' Mick brought Ma and me chips one Saturday night. I was tidying after; the smelly papers were all over the sofa. Under them a wallet—Mick's wallet. I was only looking in it; his feet made no noise coming up behind me.

We're in Cathy's garden. Weeds are green ('Most of them'). Flowers are colours ('Well, most of them'). 'No! That's an alpine Tina,' Cathy calls over. 'No! Not that either.' There's a big sponge under my knees; the sun is hot on the back of my neck. I almost laugh at a bird singing a silly song—cheep-cheep, cheepity, cheep. 'Smell these.' Cathy runs her hands up some purple flowers, then holds them to me. 'You know the lady I was telling you about, who I lived with. They remind me of her. Lavender talc—you could always smell it in her house.'

The pile of weeds gets bigger. 'You've done really well, Tina. I'll get my scissors and cut you some flowers for your room. Brighten it…' Someone is opening the gate. He's taller, older than me. They are laughing. He says not to hug him to death. 'Tina. This is Matthew. He lived here for a while.' She is still hugging him. '*This is your room, Matthew,*' she would have said. '*Make yourself at home.*'

Above the bed I can get my finger under an edge of wallpaper. Not much comes off. The next bit is better—a long skinny strip. Each bit is different. There's a knock on the door, and Cathy comes in. 'Tea's ready… what … what *on earth*?' She stares slowly around the room. I look out the window, past the pink and yellow flowers in the jug. She sighs, loudly. 'Come and get your tea.'

I'm going to see Ma on Sunday. Cathy says she'll

take me, if that's okay with me. She'll wait outside in the car. A knot ties in my belly. I know what it'll be like. Ma's eyes won't be bloodshot any more, but her hands will shake; they never shake like that at home. She'll hug me too hard, and if I cry, she'll tell me I'm soft, I need to harden up, and if I don't, she doesn't like that either. She'll say, 'S'pose you like this new place? Better than being with your old ma.'

'That's settled then, I'll take you,' Cathy says again. 'Now, remember you promised to help me make a cake. If you can't have cake on your birthday when can you have it?'

Turning on the mixer is the best bit. Flour floats out, over our hair, our aprons. 'Not full speed, Tina!' Cathy laughs. We eat all the sticky stuff left in the bowl. 'Now for the icing.'

I get to turn on the mixer again. White sugar clouds puff over us. She hands me a tiny bottle of red stuff. 'Just a dro…' But the bottle's already empty.

'Not to worry… It'll look fine when it's on.' She's trying not to laugh at the red icing.

'You're too fat anyway!' I shout. 'Look at you, fat-fat-fat!'

She turns her back to me, going over to the sink. Her voice is strange, 'Why… why don't you go outside and play. I'll wash up.'

She's not there when I come in again. I run up the stairs, flinging open her bedroom door. She's asleep, lying on her back on the bed. Her mouth is open. There's photos in frames on the dressing table. Matthew is small and skinny like me. Cathy says something, but doesn't wake up. I lie down beside her, on the bed. Her chest rises up, then down; up, then down.

When I wake my head is on a soft pillow. It rises up, then down; up then down.

There's lots of envelopes on the mat. Inside are cards—*Happy Birthday Cathy! Enjoy your cake, no one makes as scrummy cake as you! Lots of love from…*

We're on our second slice. I can't wait any longer. 'For me?' Cathy opens the paper bag. 'Oh…' She holds the soap up to her nose, looking at me for too long. 'Lavender.' She smiles, blinking. 'You remembered.'

On Saturday we go to the supermarket. Cathy lifts a tiny bottle from a shelf. 'This is to make lemon icing.' She nudges me with her elbow. 'That's *lemon*, not *yellow*, Tina.' I nudge her back. 'Do you want to get something, to give to your mum tomorrow?' she asks, and I instantly tighten. 'Does she like chocolates… Everyone likes them. They're in the next aisle. I'll catch you up.'

I walk past the boxes of chocolates; keep on walking. Ma will get out soon. It's always the same; I go to see her, and then they let her out. My belly starts to twist.

Someone is too close behind me.

'Where's your ma?'

I freeze.

His hand grabs my shoulder, turning me around.

'She's never at the flat. Where is she?'

I can see Cathy coming behind him, her forehead wrinkling; she walks quicker.

'Were she took in again?'

'Is everything okay, Tina?'

Cathy looks at Mick instead of me as she says it.

He pushes out his chest, tries to outstare her, but she moves her head closer to his, giving him as good back.

'Tell her I were round,' he says, walking away.

In the car, Cathy asks again, am I okay. I'm picturing Ma's face if she knew he was back, picturing how she cried when he left; now she'll smile, smoothing her hair down over her cheek, the way she does, over and over, to cover the scar, from the time she 'had it comin.'

That night, I'm lying on my bed in the dark, my fingers moving through the coins from my lunchbox sales. I need to wait til late, have to make sure no one sees where I go, that way they'll never find me. I can hear Cathy below in the kitchen, opening and shutting cupboard doors. At last she goes to bed.

At midnight I get up, go downstairs. I'm putting biscuits in my pocket when the kitchen door opens. I freeze. Cathy walks past me to the fridge. 'I can't sleep either. Will we have some hot milk?'

She switches on the pan on the cooker. 'Will you get out the mugs, Tina?' I reach towards the usual cupboard door, but she says, 'Your one's in the cupboard at the end.'

Inside is the sponge I knelt on in the garden, and the mug I like with the pandas on it. And my pink lunch box, and the tiny yellow bottle from the supermarket. Taped to the back of the door *Tina's things* is wrote on a square of paper.

'You did such a good job in the garden,' says Cathy, 'I was thinking, maybe you'd like a Saturday job? I could do with the help, and it's only fair you'd get paid.' She pauses. 'And if it's raining you can help me bake instead, it's never any fun baking on your own. Saturday can be my treat day; it's very important when you're on a diet to have a treat now and then.'

We drink our milk. 'Night then,' says Cathy. 'You put whatever else you want in your cupboard. It'll always be here for you, Tina.'

I stay sat at the kitchen table; opposite me is the back door. Time to go. I stand up, step towards the door. Another step, and then I see the key's not in the lock. *Climb out a window, Tina,* says a voice in my head… my cheeks are wet, I stand and stand…

My feet finally move, over to the cupboard, opening it, and taking out the sponge, holding it to my nose— there are tiny purple petals stuck to it. I lie down on the floor, and put my head on it, breathing it in, and closing my eyes…

Just for a while.

Red

It was her fault.

She had asked herself in, cheerful and smiling, as if it would rub off on me, as if I'd been waiting for someone like her to put me right.

Not good to be around, she should have known that by the way I looked, but she was already through the door.

So you see, it was her own fault.

'Just thought I'd pop round to see you,' she said. 'Sarah gave me your address...'

They were golfing chums, she had told me, when we first met at Sarah's house.

Now she wanted to get chummy with me. Cheer me up.

'This is for you. It almost didn't make it intact,' she added with a laugh, reaching me the cake tin in her hands. 'I only turned my back for a moment and the boys had the lid off, you know what teenagers are like...'

No, I don't.

Her brow wrinkled as she realised what she had said. 'It's a Victoria Sandwich,' she went on with a smile, as if this made up for putting her foot in it.

The cake tin was heavy; I almost let it slip through my hands to the floor, to show I didn't want it or her in my house.

She watched me set it on the table, then glanced

around the kitchen, frowning. This won't do, I knew she was thinking, these unwashed dishes won't do.

'Shall I put the kettle on?' she asked.

No.

She rolled up the sleeves of her cardigan. Ran the tap. Talked as she washed-up. Chattered to her new chum.

'I thought we could maybe see a film next week…'

No.

'And there's a good Chinese, maybe you know it, beside the cinema. We could…'

No.

She paused, after drying a glass, turned her head, 'I understand how you're feeling. I know you think I don't…but I do. I really do.'

That was when it happened.

It was her fault.

I didn't ask her to do the dishes. Didn't want her to say she understood, didn't want her to step towards me, reaching out.

She shouldn't have tried to touch me. I only pushed her, just a little push to stop her touching me. She stumbled backwards, against the bench, onto the glass she'd just dried. It shattered under her arm.

She had wanted to clear up the mess, and now she was making more, dripping blood everywhere.

If only Sarah was here… But it probably looked worse than it was. It was just the amount of blood, on her, on the bench and sink.

A bandage, that was what she needed. There was one

somewhere, in a cupboard.

She sat, rummaging with her good hand in her bag, phoning Sarah, asking in a high, distressed voice as if it was a major tragedy, for her to please come quickly.

A bandage, a bowl of water and kitchen roll. She flinched when I touched her. Blood now on the table as well.

'I need a doctor.' A tear trickled down her cheek. 'Stitches.'

The kitchen roll soaked red.

'I won't tell Sarah that you… I'll say… I broke a glass washing up.'

It was just a little push.

'I know you're not yourself. How could you be?'

More kitchen roll, then the bandage… redness still seeping through.

Looked like she'd tried to slit her wrist. *She's usually so cheerful,* I'd whisper to Sarah.

'What's funny?' Annoyed face. 'My being hurt amuses you?'

Being cross didn't suit her, cheeriness was more her style, dimpled her cheeks when she smiled. She looked older now, more lines on her forehead.

'Do you think I've nothing better to do?' Raised voice. 'Than come here and get no response!'

Where are you, Sarah?

More tears… 'I didn't mean that. I'm sorry.'

Over to the sink, to empty the bowl of red water. Broken glass on the bench, on the floor.

'I didn't talk either… not for weeks.'

Blood on the dishes, on the drainer.

'Not talking feels good, doesn't it? You are never going to speak again. No one can make you.'

Concentrate on washing-up.

'Did Sarah ever tell you about my first husband?'

Put soapy water into a mug, swirl it around, rinse, place back on drainer.

'It was the start of our honeymoon. He went swimming. He always swam at home… But this was an unknown sea, with unknown currents.'

Concentrate on washing-up.

'It happened a long time ago. But I vividly remember how I felt, the way you are feeling now…'

Hurry up, Sarah.

'You think it's different for you. I can understand that. It must be even harder when…'

Don't say it!

'…there's a child involved.'

I'm not listening.

'I blamed myself, for letting him swim… As if I could have stopped him.'

I'm not listening!

'You blame yourself, don't you? You think if only you had kept her at home that day.'

'Don't wanna go.' All I'd to say was, Okay, I'll phone Daddy, just made that simple phone call. Should have thought—Why doesn't she want to go? Just that simple question. That's all I had to ask myself. Why?

'But you mustn't blame yourself. You thought she would be safe. Anyone would have.'

Why is it taking you so long to get here, Sarah?

'She was a beautiful child.'

They wouldn't let me see her, wouldn't let me see my beautiful child.

'At the party... remember the Christmas party at Sarah's?'

Stop talking. Please stop talking! Where are you, Sarah?

'I said to her, "That's a very pretty dress, Lucy. Red is my favourite colour." And she said, "Me too."'

It was just to make her shut up. The shard of glass in my hand.

That was when it happened.

It was her fault. She screamed; tried to force it from my hand. Cut her good hand, cut mine. What did she think I was going to do, cut my own throat? Cut hers?

It didn't hurt yet—the gash in my palm.

I wanted to ask, would Lucy have suffered? But I couldn't speak. They asked, did I know he was taking anti-depressants? No, of course I didn't. How would I? He was my ex-husband. I tried to say it, Ex, but nothing came out. They asked, did he not usually wear a seatbelt? Did he not usually put Lucy's seat belt on?

My hand throbbed.

Of course she would have suffered.

I closed my fist, dug my fingers into my palm.

The sound of a car outside—Sarah. Her friend rushed to the door, turned around when a safe distance from me. 'I... I was only trying...'

My head nodded, I even managed a smile, now she was leaving. Closed the door after her. Locked it.

Then sat at the table. Blood on it. Darkening now as it dried. Dark red.

Lucy was wearing her red dungarees that day. But I could change that. I pictured her in a dress, her blue one with the white flowers, sitting in the car. And she had her seatbelt on. He didn't, but she did. She watched as the windscreen broke around him, watched him rise up into the air. Bye, bye Daddy. She was still sitting in the car, waiting for me. Hurry up, Mummy. It's cold.

Specks of blood on the cake tin on the table.

It was her fault she got hurt. Someone had to take the blame. I didn't ask her to come here.

It was my fault… All I had to ask was—*Why? Why don't you want to go with Daddy?*

Shard of glass on the floor beside me.

Gazed at it.

Picked it up.

Both wrists—Swiped. Swiped.

Then rubbed my hands around my neck, up my throat, over my face. *Look Lucy, Mummy's just like you.*

Red was her favourite colour.

Someone at the other side of the door. Handle moved down and up.

My name being called. Handle down and up.

'Open the door!'

Sarah.

'I shouldn't have told her where you lived. She said…

she said you… Please, let me in.'

My head was too heavy to hold up… slowly lowered it down, cheek against the table. Surface was sticky. Dark and sticky. Red was Lucy's favourite colour.

'Help's on its way, they'll be here any minute. C'mon, open the door, *please.*'

You don't have to go Lucy, if you don't want to.

Sarah was calling my name again, 'I *really* need you to open…' but her voice was fading now, or maybe it was me who was moving further away.

Hurry up, Mummy. It's cold.

Won't be long now, sweetheart. Mummy's coming.

Basket of Eggs

I'm eighty-eight ye know.

Really? You don't look it.

And ye got m full name, didnae ye?

She nods.

John Herbert William Patterson.

So, Mr Patterson, maybe we could move on to…

Did ye writ it doon?

Sorry?

M name. Did ye get it all doon?

Remember Mr Patterson, I explained about this little machine, how it's recording everything we…

P-A-T-T-E-R-S-O-N… Ye're a nice writer, I'll gie ye that. Nineteen twenty-four, that were the year I were born.

In this cottage?

Aye. It hasnae changed much. I know what ye're thinkin, that ye wouldnae want tae live here.

She doesn't know what to say because he's right, there is the overpowering smell of damp for a start; she can even feel it, cold and clammy on her skin.

When we was wee, we'd nae lectric, nae runnin water.

How many…

Six o us there were. Six weans.

And your father, I believe, worked for Harland and Wolff?

He did. Worked at the docks a his life.

So he… stayed in Belfast?

Well, he'd hardly travel frae here.

No. No, of course not.

Done what were needed on the land o a Saturday.

Have you much land?

Five acre, or there aboot.

I suppose you get walkers up the glen?

The Yanks take pictures o me, sittin ootside.

Oh… yes. They'd be tracing their ancestors in Antrim. Maybe you have relations–

Ye'd think they'd ne'er seen a cottage afore. They want tae take me picture, if I'm sittin ootside, or standin in the durway.

She tries to get more comfortable, moving position on her chair, the seat of which seems to be collapsed; from the slumped way he is sitting his is probably the same. Wood is burning in the fireplace, a few small logs, not enough to warm the cold air.

And your father, as you said, worked at the shipyard. You wouldn't have seen much of him then?

He'd lodgin's wi a great aunt.

I live in Belfast. Actually, near where your father worked. In the Titanic Quarter.

Ye dinnae look oul enough.

What do you… Oh no, of course I wasn't *on* the Titanic. I said I lived…

His shoulders are shaking with mirth.

Ha, ha, very funny.

Even I'm nae oul enough.

With this being the Titanic's centenary year, I'll be reporting…

On the unsinkable ship.

Yes.

That sank.

Well… yes.

He worked on her ye know, m father.

Really? That's…

As a welder. When she went doon, ye couldnae mention her name after.

He took it hard then? Oh! What's that? Oh!

Her chair, something is under her chair! It moves again… a mouse? Or a rat!

It's on'y a hin. Go on, ge oot wi ye. Shoo!

Right… Ahem, do you have any other…

Just the hins. We'd a cow when we was wee. M mother milked it. Ye ever tried it?

M-milking? Erm, no, I can't say that…

How many weans hae you?

Me? No, I haven't any children…Well, not yet. I'm…

Frigit?

She can feel the heat rising up her neck, blushing over her face.

More career orientated. Were you… are you married, Mr Patterson?

Nae, I wasnae ever married…There were a girl I liked… but she didnae like me, the way I liked her.

Right… Okay. Actually, Mr Patt–

Jack.

Maybe, we could move on to…

Ye dinnae want tae leave it tae late ha'ing weans. M mother were tae oul when she'd Eliz'beth. She took the monia straight after, hadnae the strength tae fight it.

This is your sister Elizabeth you mean. The one who… disappeared?

She were tae oul, when she'd Eliz'beth, didnae even last the year.

Who looked after her, the baby I mean, who looked after all of...

We looked after oorsel'es.

But...

Walter were eighteen. He were the ouldest. They woulda taken us, the social people, but Walter were oul enough, at eighteen.

But how did you manage with your father working in Belfast?

We'd the farm tae look after.

You milked the cow?

Aye. And we'd a couple o sows. If we were lucky we'd ge a good litter frae them in the year. An we'd a few ewes as weel.

Did you grow any crops?

Prataes.

Pardon? Oh, you mean potatoes. And what else did you...

It's tae caul up here fer much else. Just onions an neeps, that's all would dae. Eliz'beth tried lettuce, but it didnae dae.

And Elizabeth lived here with you? Did she ever live anywhere else?

She went wi m father sometimes tae Belfast, stayed in his aunt's lodgin's, helped oot wi the washin an cookin.

But she was here that day in June?

He gazes silently at her, eyes still those of a much younger man, the first thing she noticed, how bright they were.

Mr Patt... Jack? Did you hear what I said? Was she

here…

The day afore her thirtieth birthday.

That was the day she disappeared? That was the second of June nineteen seventy-two?

He nods.

Can you remember what you thought at the time; had you any idea…

I were in the back field. I always coom in at twelve fer somethin tae eat. The eggs were oon the table, in her basket oon the table… but she werenae there.

And you didn't see anything, hear anything, when you were in the field?

Nae.

Somewhere as remote as this, you would have heard it, if there'd been a car, a vehicle…

She went oot tae collect the eggs like she always doon. I went up tae the back field, an when I came back she werenae there.

And no one passed her on the road; there were no witnesses…

Nae.

And you never saw her again?

He sighs, shaking his head.

But she's not on the list.

What dae ye mean?

Of 'The Disappeared'. Remember that's why I'm here; I'm writing a report about the latest development.

Ye said ye wanted tae ask me aboot Eliz'beth.

Yes, that's right, because she's now connected with the list of Northern Ireland's 'Disappeared'.

He doesn't seem to understand what she is saying, his

confusion evident in his eyes. But he knows about his sister; she isn't saying anything he wouldn't already have been told by the police.

Mr Patterson... Jack... Are you okay? I can switch off the recorder. We can have a break.

Of course she's nae on the list. They was people the IRA took, their oon kind.

The dislike, hatred even in his voice, surprises her.

You mean Catholics?

Eliz'beth had nothin tae dae wi them. She knew better.

You don't think they were victims, 'The Disappeared' of the Troubles? They were abducted and killed...

There's nae smoke wi'oot fire.

Mary McNeary. Have you heard of that name, Jack?

He looks away from her, towards the fireplace.

A mother of eight. A widow. They took her because she helped a wounded soldier. A Catholic helping a British soldier. Like your sister, she just seemed to vanish one day in the seventies. Her children were taken into care; they found out only recently where her body was buried.

He is shaking his head.

She were one o them though... Dinnae sigh like that at me. M sister were a good un. She looked after us, always had the dinner oon the table.

Why do you think her remains have been found... where they've been found?

The recorder whirrs in the long silence.

Why would she have been buried with one of the listed? With a man the IRA have now admitted to taking in nineteen seventy-two, and have released information about where he's buried.

She'd nothin tae do wi scum. I woulda known. Ye think I wouldnae hae known?

He was my uncle.

What do ye...

The man buried with your sister.

But...

Seamus Quigly.

Ge...ge oot...ge oot o...

He struggles to get up from his chair, his face flushed.

You're going to shoo me out like one of your hens?

He stands tottering on his feet, for an awful moment she thinks he is going to fall, but then he sits back down, slumped forward in his chair.

Are you okay?...Will I get you a glass of water?

Ye lied tae me, ye tol me yer name were...

Stewart. And it is. It is Alison Stewart. I'm hardly going to have the same surname as the man my aunt married. I'm a Protestant; I can see that's what you want to know. It was a mixed marriage, my aunt and Seamus Quigly.

Ye tol me ye were a reporter.

I am! You can ring the office, speak to my boss. There's my phone. Do you want me to get him on the line? Look, I've turned off the recorder. You can speak to my boss, he'll...

It isnae her. It isnae Eliz'beth onyway.

He straightens up in his chair; she can see his conviction in this statement.

What do you mean?

It isnae her they found. Eliz'beth knew tae stay clear o fenians.

They identified her by her dental records.

He shakes his head.

Seamus lived in Belfast. He and my aunt had a corner shop. You said Elizabeth stayed sometimes with your relations in Belfast.

It isnae her.

They said… the IRA said he was an informer, that was why they took him, but my aunt denies it. She says she would have known… But then she didn't know about Elizabeth.

It isnae her.

He was a good-looking man, my uncle. I can show you a photograph. Maybe, he and Elizabeth planned to run away. That day in June, maybe she'd walked down the road from here to meet him, down the side of the glen. He had a van for doing deliveries for the shop. But they didn't get to where they were going. He vanished that day, both he and the van.

He shakes his head.

Like your sister did that same day.

It isnae her.

But then again, perhaps she didn't know him, maybe they weren't running away together. Your sister could just have been out walking, along the road, and she saw them abducting him, and so they had to take her as well. She'd have been a witness.

He is still shaking his head.

It's been forty years. Do you not want to finally lay her to rest?

I tol ye. Eliz'beth wouldnae…

What happened to her then?

He looks blankly back at her.

What happened that day?

I…I dinnae know. She… she'd brough in the eggs…

He points towards the other side of the room.

There's her basket. See, over yonder, hangin on the rafter.

She disappeared the same day as Seamus Quigly. She's been found, buried in a bog, with Seamus Quigly.

I've kept the basket, fer when she comes back. She wouldnae hae onythin tae dae wi fenians. When she cooms back, ye can ask her yerself where she's been, what she's been doin.

He is trying to sit erect in his broken chair, clinging to the hope his sister is still alive. She shouldn't have come, but her aunt has waited forty years to lay Seamus to rest, and now he's been found buried with someone else it throws up even more questions.

Ye've had a wasted journey comin here, noo ye know it isnae Eliz'beth.

Are any of your other brothers and sisters…

There's on'y me and Eliz'beth left.

I'm sorry if I've brought back painful memories. I'll not take up any more of your time. Thank you for talking to me.

They want me tae go into one o them homes, ye know fer oul people. But what'll happen when Eliz'beth cooms back? There'd be nae one here… an me and the hins are doin alright. I'm eighty-eight, ye know.

She nods.

Eliz'beth knew tae stick wi her oon kind.

She sits forward, preparing to stand.

M father tol us when we was wee what fenians were like, tol us how sleekit they were, warned us nae tae trust em, that they'd take the land, take everythin frae us when they got a united Ireland.

Is that what *you* believe?

Well... I've been thinkin lately, he didnae like onyone much, m father.

For a moment she thinks he is joking, but he is gazing seriously at her.

Why are ye smilin?

What would your father have made of the Good Friday agreement?

He frowns, perplexed, and she changes her question.

What did *you* make of it?

Well... I dinnae know... what I dae know, is I couldnae stand them chuckly brothers.

Paisley and McGuinness?

Aye.

Why not?

They didnae hae tae cosy up tae each other like they done.

It's peaceful now though.

Aye, it's peaceful up here alright.

I meant in Northern Ireland.

Oh, aye. Aye, it is.

I'll shake your hand then before I go, Mr Patterson... Jack.

Hae ye a picture?

It takes a moment for her to understand.

You mean of my uncle?

Aye.

She lifts up her bag from beside her chair, rummaging in it…

She coom back frae Belfast wi her head in the clouds, couldnae mind what ye tol her… but that doesnae mean…

At last she finds the photograph, but he doesn't take it from her outstretched hand, gazing up at the cottage rafters.

Will ye reach it doon?

She walks across the room, bringing down the basket.

Thon's her scarf inside. She'd wear it when it were caul, tae collect the eggs.

It's pretty.

Look un'er it.

Oh… where did you get this?

It were long after she'd goon, years after. M father were passed on by then. The hin shed needed fixed. I found it behin a stone in the wall. Is it him?

She sits down again, comparing the two photographs.

Yes, it's him.

He closes his eyes, the colour draining from his face.

Are you okay?

She leans forward, touching his hand, and he opens his eyes.

It woulda kilt m father… if he hadnae already passed oon.

He slowly shakes his head.

Ye know, him bein one o them. An married tae boot…

His hand is trembling under hers.

It gets lonely up here, on yer oon. She's no comin back then, Eliz'beth?

She gently squeezes his hand.

It were the day afore her thirtieth birthday. She went

oot tae collect the eggs, like she always doon. I coom in at twelve fer somethin tae eat. The eggs were oon the table…in her basket oon the table… but she werenae there. She jus…

His head droops, and he stays silent, as though unable to continue. But then he looks up at her again.

… dis'ppeared.

Catalina

14, Heyburn Close.
   20th August 2018

Dear Gerald,

I know you will be surprised I am writing to you, but I can't bring myself to tell you this over the telephone. Bad news travels fast, they say, and I don't want you to hear about me from someone else. I doubt you would believe it. '*Norris?*' I can imagine you gasping. 'No, that can't be right, Norris would never do that!'

It began one Friday, on my way home from work. The bus pulled up at the stop, and the girl standing in front of me (petite, with long brown hair tied in a pony tail) turned back her head. 'I sit with you?' she asked, her eyes darting beyond me to the rest of the queue. Her complexion was pale, and I guessed she was in her early twenties. 'On bus, please I sit with you?' she repeated, and I could see desperation in her eyes.

Once on the bus, she explained, voice trembling, 'He… not stay away,' indicating with a small movement of her hand, that this person she referred to was sitting somewhere in front. Her obvious fear of him made me recall an item lately on the news about a young woman who had been stalked and killed by her ex-fiancé, who'd had a history of violence she knew nothing about. My companion asked then, if she could get off with me at my stop.

Again, I didn't hesitate, the horrible news story still

on my mind.

What would you have done, Gerald? I'm guessing the same as me. 'Too nice,' wasn't that what your ex-wife accused you of.

The girl clung to my arm as we got off the bus, letting 'him' see she was… what though? He was hardly going to believe I was her new boyfriend—partner, whatever the name is these days. There was the age difference for a start. I still haven't got around to joining the gym Gerald, and the bathroom mirror is unforgiving to my fifty-one-year-old face, as are the scales.

Unlike the slip of a thing at my side, and Catalina (as I was to discover she was called) clutched tighter to my arm, informing me that 'he' had also got off the bus.

So, now I was in a dilemma, and the thought went through my mind to confront him, because as we learnt at school, didn't we Gerald, bullies are usually cowards in disguise, but Catalina was extremely agitated, hurrying forward, still holding me by the arm so that we were almost running along the pavement.

Once outside my house, I acted on the spur of the moment, steering Catalina towards the front door, quickly opening and closing it behind us. My chest hurt, and my breathing was quick and shallow as I tried to regain my composure, with Catalina standing wide-eyed in my hall, gazing at me with an expression of fear and astonishment.

When I could speak, I told her not to be afraid, realising the poor girl probably thought she had escaped one tormentor, only to be accosted by another.

I said I would make us a cup of tea, then we'd check if the coast was clear. She frowned, confused, and as I tried to explain that *coast* didn't always mean *the sea*, she smiled.

The lighting up of her face transformed it, showing how pretty she was, and we stood, smiling at each other for several moments, before I pulled myself together and went into the kitchen to put the kettle on.

As she sipped her tea, she explained how she had come from Poland to legally work here 'with paper' as she put it, but the factory where she had found employment closed down, which meant she couldn't pay her rent, and that was when 'he', her eyes grew fearful again, 'help me. Kind... to start.'

When it was time for her to go, she reached out her hand, taking mine; I thought she was going to shake it, but instead she held it against her cheek, giving me a brave smile. I opened the front door feeling as if I was sending a child out into the jungle.

She paused on the step, gazing up and down the street. In the act of stepping forward she froze. 'What is it? Is it him?' and as she shrank back into the house, I caught a glimpse of him. I couldn't see his face distinctly as he had on a hooded top, but I noted he was stocky as he disappeared.

So, what to do? *Go to the police, Norris*, I know you are thinking Gerald, and that was also my intention, but Catalina shook her head, 'Make him... angry more.' She looked so petrified I couldn't risk it.

The guest bedroom is still the same Gerald, as you know the bed is rather hard, and the damp along the back wall has got worse, but Catalina seemed pleasantly overwhelmed when she saw it, which made me wonder what her living conditions were like.

It was just meant to be for the one night, but a week later I found myself looking forward to coming home, the inviting aroma of dinner cooking as I came through the front door. My house as you will recall Gerald is moderately neat and tidy, but Catalina transformed it, every surface spotless and shining, the carpets vacuumed daily.

I know what people might assume Gerald, but Catalina continued to sleep in the spare room. When I went to work each morning, we closed the curtains and I locked her in the house. This was at her request; she said it made her feel safe, a shadow passing over her face.

You've probably already foreseen what happened next Gerald, it even seemed inevitable at the time that he would come looking for her, and when the doorbell rang long and insistently one evening Catalina and I looked at each other, the dread in her eyes no doubt a reflection of mine.

As I mentioned before, he was thick-set, and up close I could see the bulge of his arm muscles through his sleeves, but from a menace point of view, it was the unsavoury aspect of his face that was most alarming, particularly his shifty eyes, looking beyond me into the house.

He accused me of imprisoning Catalina, 'makin her yer skivvy' as he put it, and if I didn't release her he would go to the police. The word 'slave' was even spoken, which set off alarm bells, having recently heard it used on the news in connection to an arrest. Or, he said—and no doubt you'll also have predicted this Gerald—we could come to an arrangement.

I had until the end of the week to get him the money.

As I closed the front door with a trembling hand, the possibility rushed through my mind—*What if they were in it together, what if they'd set me up?*—but as I saw Catalina crouched in a corner of the living room with her head in her hands, I knew it wasn't true.

I hurried across the room to her with words of reassurance that he was gone, and she buried her face in my chest, sobbing her little heart out. I told her now, we *had* to tell the police, but she begged me not, becoming even more distraught, and I held her in my arms, trying to soothe her.

And this led to... please don't judge me, Gerald, I didn't take advantage, in fact she was the one...

The following day I kept making mistakes at the office, my thoughts preoccupied with Catalina of course and our new intimacy, and what I was to do about the blackmail. At lunchtime, I took the rest of the day off, heading for the bank. I know you are raising your eyebrows Gerald, but I didn't regret my decision as I sat on the bus, in fact the thought of Catalina waiting at home made me smile, and I hummed as I approached my house.

The living room window was wide open.

I halted.

He had broken in—my heart was pounding—he

was inside the house with her!

I fumbled with my key, trying to open the front door as quietly as possible, standing still in the hall, listening… I could hear something now… there it was again, from the kitchen.

I picked up the bronze statue on the sideboard, moving closer…

The fury that rushed through me when I saw him— I have never experienced before Gerald, or wish to again—when I saw him forcing himself on her, and it was so overwhelming it obliterated any rational thought about my actions. One moment I was standing at the kitchen door, and the next, I remember kneeling over his inert body, praying he wasn't dead.

No doubt you are gasping, Gerald. But once you've had time to think about everything I have told you, I hope that you'll have understanding in your heart, which brings me to the second purpose of this letter.

I need a character reference for my court hearing.

I tried to ask my boss, but instead found myself requesting extended leave from the office. Now, in the mornings my alarm clock no longer rings, but I waken anyway, and for a few seconds everything is normal again before my spirits sink as I remember I no longer go to work. I spend my days indoors, the curtains closed, the door locked. In hiding, just like… They will have read in the paper—everyone at the office, the neighbours—that I've been charged with Grievous Bodily Harm.

I pass the hours thinking of Catalina, picturing her smiling at me that first day in the hall, and I was about to add I hope she'll return to me, that she'll somehow escape from his clutches…

But I need to be honest with you Gerald, and I have been… apart from how I found them on the kitchen floor… I find this difficult to write… She had her legs wound around his back, her hands in his hair, softly moaning.

I'm sorry for misleading you Gerald, but I was describing what my eyes told me was happening at the time, that he was attacking her.

Now, I realise this was because I was unable to bear the truth.

No fool like an old fool, is what I tell myself during my long days and nights, and is no doubt what you are thinking Gerald. You said to me once, after your divorce, that the only woman you should trust is your mother. I should have paid that more heed.

The odd thing is, despite everything… although, maybe I shouldn't say this Gerald as it sounds insane…

I'm glad that Catalina chose me in the bus queue, because the few weeks I spent with her have been the happiest of my life.

Your old friend,
Norris

Thud

She watched them as they fed the hens. The taller man made a clucking noise with his tongue, throwing grain and scraps of food in wide arcs. The smaller one quickly emptied his bucket and started collecting eggs. He knew where to look, among clumps of long grass, under a bush.

They weren't dressed like farmers; both wore worn, faded raincoats and trousers that were too short, even the small man's. It was their shoes that gave them away, she knew farmers didn't wear plimsolls.

The tall man watched the birds squawking and fighting over the food, before also collecting eggs. He did it slowly, examining each carefully, then placing it in his bucket. Was he looking at their size; colour? He stood, gazing vacantly, as though forgetting what he was in the act of doing. The other man walked over, putting a hand on his arm and he started collecting again.

Emma stepped from behind the hen shed. The movement caught their attention. They stared; she stared, like two species of animal encountering for the first time.

'Hello,' she said, lifting her hand. She took another step forward. 'I hope you don't mind... They gave me directions in the village.'

The tall man turned away, looking for eggs again. The small one held out his bucket in her direction. 'What have you for us?'

It took a moment for Emma to work out what he meant. 'No, I don't want eggs. I'm not here to barter.'

She moved closer to him. His face was lined, weather beaten; it was difficult to judge his age. She guessed around fifty.

'I'm a journalist. Can I ask a few questions? I'm doing a feature on alternative lifestyles. You guys are just what I'm looking for.'

The tall man came over. His bucket was full to the brim with eggs. He looked down at them as he spoke. 'What you give us?'

Emma explained again, 'No, I'm not here to barter. Although, that's one of the things I want to ask you about. If you could give me a few minutes of your time…'

This last sentence was spoken to the men's backs as they walked away. Emma followed, her shoes catching on the rough stones. Dilapidated sheds with tin roofs lined each side of the yard.

They stopped beside a wooden bench, sitting, lifting the eggs out of the buckets at their feet and cleaning them with a cloth.

'I'm Emma, by the way,' she said. 'I'll pay you for an interview.'

They didn't respond, and she glanced through the open shed door next to her. At the far wall was what appeared to be an electric cooker. A fridge against another wall was also rusted brown. On a small table were mugs and plates.

She turned back to the men, watching them fill cardboard cartons with six eggs each. The tall man looked up, gazing with a blank expression at the yard beyond Emma. His eyes were an unusual colour—grey flecked with green. The other man touched his arm and he resumed work.

'I believe you're brothers.'

This was one of the few things that people in the village knew about them. They didn't lift their heads from their work.

Once the egg boxes were filled, they placed them carefully inside plastic bags, and the brothers carried them back down the yard.

Emma followed. They made their way along a narrow, overgrown lane and onto the road where she had left her car.

'Can I give you a lift, guys? Are you going to the village?'

They didn't turn their heads, walking past her car.

'Do you mind if I tag along?' she asked. The small man glanced back at her, but didn't speak.

She had to walk quickly to keep up. The tall man had a limp, she'd noticed earlier, and it got more pronounced as the journey continued. The small brother took short, quick strides, glancing back at her again as they rounded a bend in the road.

Little and Lame.

She watched the backs of the two men walking in front of her. Lame was round-shouldered. How did someone with a limp like that move so quickly?

Emma walked faster, closing the gap. 'They told me in the village that one of you used to be a car mechanic?'

Little's step faltered. So it was him. Lame looked

anxiously at his brother. Her words had upset them both. They would know she was lying, that she didn't hear this information in the village. They increased their pace, trying to leave her behind. Her heels clicked faster on the road, keeping up.

They reached the village. Lame opened the door of the only shop, the one where Emma had asked directions. The man behind the counter nodded at Little as he set the bags of eggs onto the counter. The brothers collected things from the shelves—bread, cheese, tea bags, a few tins. The strain of Emma's presence showed in the hurried, jerky movements of their hands. The man at the counter put their groceries in the bags the eggs had been in, nodding again to the brothers.

Emma followed them back along the road. 'So, what now guys? This is really good of you, letting me hang out.'

They walked quicker, and she let them leave her behind. When she reached her car, they were no longer in sight. She opened the car door, getting in, leaning back her head, closing her eyes. She had to decide what to do, now that the search was over.

Now that she had found him.

The yard was silent. The door into the shed where they lived was still open, the way they had left it when they took the eggs to the village. Emma stepped inside. It didn't smell bad, the way she expected, just damp. A cooker, a fridge, a table, two chairs, some crockery, that was it. There was no sink in the small room. The concrete floor was swept clean. Emma walked towards a door in one of the walls.

'*Hello?*'

She waited.

Then put her hand on the door handle, opening it.

It took a moment for her eyes to adjust to the gloom. There was no one inside. Two beds lined the walls of the tiny room, blankets folded neatly on top. The only light was from a window about a foot square.

Outside again, Emma looked inside the other sheds. One contained farm implements—wheelbarrows, spades, buckets. The next door she opened gave her a start, even though she had been expecting to find an animal.

The goat turned its head, also startled. She almost laughed; their lifestyle was so predictable. It seemed well cared for; clean straw piled thickly on the floor. The animal's brown hide was gleaming. It annoyed her, that it was well looked after.

She opened the shed door wider, standing beyond view. The goat walked outside. She shut the door behind it, and it walked across the yard, towards the lane. She chased after, waving her arms. It trotted down the lane, disappearing from sight.

Emma burst out laughing, she couldn't help herself. When it subsided, she stood still, listening.

What was that noise?

She walked in its direction, behind the shed in which they lived. She could see the brothers now; they were in a small field. Lame was knocking a wooden post into the ground. Little was on his knees among drills of vegetables.

'Hello again. A vegetable garden; I might have known! You guys are so self-sufficient.'

She walked along a drill. 'I've been having a look in the sheds. I see you've a goat. You really are trying to have the good life here! I don't think much of your living accommodation though. Your bedroom is like a prison cell.'

She stopped beside Little. 'If I was a journalist, which I'm not, I don't think my readers would be impressed by your lifestyle.'

He kept his back to her. She hunkered down beside him, her fingers lifting green stalks growing from the soil. 'So, what's this?'

She pulled on the stalks, bringing up something. 'Oh, it's an onion… Well, it will be when it's grown.'

Tossing it to the side, she walked on, pulling them up as she went. She threw the half-grown vegetables in Little's direction; one of them hit him on the back.

'Oh, look, I got a bigger one!' She walked towards Lame, holding it up for him to see. 'Not big enough to eat, though.' She tossed it away.

Lame tied netting to the post that he had hammered into the ground. She moved closer to him. 'Have you worked out who I am yet?'

He kept his face turned from her, his fingers fumbling with the string.

She gazed at the area of vegetables beside him. 'I know what these are.' She fingered the leafy stalks, pulling on one. A carrot, the size of her finger, came up. 'Yes, thought so. So tiny though.' She threw it to the side, pulling up the one beside it, then the next one.

Lame walked away, breaking into a run, heading towards the yard. Little watched him.

'I have to admire your loyalty.' Emma made her way over to Little again. 'But is he worth it, do you think? And where do you draw the line? What if he'd murdered someone, for example, what if that had been his crime, instead of…'

He wouldn't look at her.

'Would you still have stuck by him then?'

She moved into his line of vision. 'You know who I am, don't you?'

'What do you want?'

I need him to pay for what he did! She wanted to shout it, scream it at him. 'Why do you stick by him? You had a job. A house.'

'He's my brother.'

'But…'

'I look after him.'

He walked away from her, towards the yard. Some of the vegetables Emma had pulled up were lying in his path, and he lifted them up as he went. They would laugh about her later, at the silly girl who thought she could intimidate them by destroying a few onions.

There had been a spade, lying in one of the drills. Little heard her footstep behind him, glancing back. The spade caught him on the side of the head. He fell forward.

She hadn't hit him hard. He would get up. Any minute now he would sit up. His face was to the side; his eyes closed. She hunkered down beside him;

watching, listening. His breathing was short and laboured.

Thud… thud.

Emma glanced up, listening to the noise, trying to work out what it was. She took a last look at Little before turning away. She had to focus on what she had come for.

Thud… thud.

She walked towards the yard in the direction of the noise.

Lame was chopping logs on a block of wood.

Emma leant against a shed wall, watching. He chopped each log in two on the block, raising the axe above his head, then into two again.

The finished pile on the ground got higher.

'Do you barter firewood at the shop?'

When he didn't reply she repeated, 'Do you exchange these for food at the shop, Richard?'

He showed no emotion when she said his name, but she could see his hand was trembling as he picked up another log, placing it on the block.

Thud… thud.

He suited Lame better anyway.

'Do they know in the village that they have a rapist living among them?'

Thud… thud.

'What was it like in prison?'

Thud… thud.

'Do you think I look like my mother?'

He picked up another log, carefully placing it in

position, his eyes concentrated on it, as if Emma wasn't there.

Thud… thud.

'I think they have a right to know, in the village.' She moved forward, walking towards him. 'Do *you* want to tell them, or will I?'

The split log fell to the ground. He picked up one half, replacing it on the block, focusing on the wood as though his life depended on it.

He swung the axe.

Thud…

'Do you still see her face? Do you still hear her scream?'

He paused in the motion of lifting the axe again, his eyes, the same colour as hers, seeming to bore into her soul.

Something in them changed.

With just one hand he swung the axe.

Thud…

His scream, like nothing she had heard before.

The block turned red.

Her eyes blinked closed, but she had to look at it, at the meat-raw flesh and sinew of what was left of his hand.

She ran down the lane to her car. As she drove away her mouth opened, the noise that came out also sounded inhuman, animal-like. Was this how her mother had screamed?

This was what she had wanted, wasn't it, for him to be punished? This was what she wanted!

Her foot pressed on the accelerator, trying to get

away from the noise in the car, from the noise in her head that never went away.

The next bend of the road appeared. His hand for what he'd done—a barter, an exchange, think of it like that. The drumming in her head intensified, pressing against her skull.

The car reached the bend.

Her tyre hit the curb. The steering wheel span out of her hands. The car began turning, spinning; once, twice. She had never believed it when people said their lives flashed before them in just seconds, but hers was now; he would be at the end of it, his hand…

Instead, vacant grey eyes, flecked with green; her mother's tired voice. 'You have to stop this obsession with him. He didn't know what he was doing, Emma. He wasn't right…'

The jolt of her car hitting the curb again, then stopping.

Emma sat still, her shoulder throbbing from being flung against the door. The buzzing in her head was gone, but it would start again any second now. 'Didn't know what he was doing.' She kept repeating it. 'Didn't know what he was doing.' She reached into her pocket for her mobile.

'Ambulance… There's been an accident. His hand… He needs an ambulance.'

Three Certainties of Love

Simply being in their presence confirmed Joanna's suspicions; she could sense their unease, noticed that they didn't meet each other's eyes when she was there. But Ralph had repeatedly denied it, insisting she was mistaken (*'Joanna darling, remember my promise'*) and now she felt a fool, because he had treated her as one, as though her mind was deteriorating as well as her body. She tugged with irritation at the rug over her knees, murmuring that she was cold, knowing even this slight discomfort wounded him, that despite his faults he would take her place in this stupid wheelchair if he could.

Her husband saw her snatch at the rug covering her wasted legs, straightening it so each corner fell over her knees down to her feet, turning to her nurse, saying Ruth would bring her a cup of tea, but even this simple request was awkward in front of his wife after what she had accused him of, his voice sounding unnatural.

Ruth saw his embarrassment, also feeling it herself, but it had occurred to her that Joanna might be understanding about their situation, that she might even be pleased that her husband wouldn't be alone after she was gone. 'Yes… yes, of course, a cup of tea.'

Joanna knew the reason for her nurse's stilted words, for the colour spreading across her cheeks, also knowing her husband's interest would be a passing whim, and she thought, I should tell her because I like her, tell Ruth what a cad he is. She looked up at her husband standing beside her; he had been adamant he was innocent and look how dejected he seemed because she didn't believe him, and despite herself she reached out her hand touching his, wanting to trust him, wanting to believe he hadn't broken his promise to never let her down again.

Ralph took her hand, gazing down at her lovely face; its gauntness didn't diminish her beauty; he could see in her eyes that she still doubted him about Ruth, and the terrible thought ran through his mind. She would leave me if she wasn't in this wheelchair, she had almost before. He bent to embrace her, telling himself, no, he was wrong she would never leave him, she loved him too much, and knew how much he loved her; he told her again now as they embraced, glancing over her shoulder towards Ruth's retreating figure as he did, his eyes lingering on the curve of her hips in her uniform.

Dusk was falling like a grey gauze over the garden as Ruth made her way across the lawn to the summerhouse. She shivered, wrapping her arms around herself as she waited. She knew Ralph wasn't on his way; she could see them together in the conservatory through the French doors. Joanna must have been reading as there was an opened book on her lap on top of her rug, and why couldn't he have let her keep on reading, thought Ruth, instead of kneeling beside her, his head on her shoulder, gazing at her like a little boy desperate for attention; he would know that Ruth could see them in the lit room, know she was waiting for him in the place they had first discovered their love, and she shivered again, this time with anticipation as he was getting up. '*Hurry,*' Ruth whispered, but he was standing behind his wife's wheelchair now, his hands on her shoulders, glancing towards the doors to the garden, towards Ruth, frowning, and she knew he was desperate to get to her, and Ralph *was* agitated, although it had nothing to do with Ruth, as his hands gently kneaded his wife's shoulders, telling her she couldn't mean it, she was overtired, that was all, but she interrupted, saying that he could visit her every day.

'You can't.' Ralph was adamant. 'You can't leave me.'

'I'll be bedridden soon,' replied Joanna, and he tried to protest that it wouldn't be soon, it would be years before, but she didn't let him finish, saying she needed to be somewhere equipped.

'It's Ruth, isn't it,' he blurted, 'that's what this is about, you think that she and I…'

'Ralph, my darling, my mind is made up.' This is about what's best for me, she thought, regardless of Ralph or anyone else, and she patted his hand on her shoulder, knowing he was struggling to come to terms with it, turning her head towards the black night at the other side of the French doors, gazing at the garden she couldn't see, that she would deeply miss, and unknown to her, Ruth gazed back at them from the summerhouse, watched as Ralph knelt again at the side of the wheelchair, this time putting his head on his wife's lap, and as she followed the slow stroke of Joanna's hand smoothing his hair, it occurred to her that Ralph would never leave Joanna because she was an invalid, even though he didn't love his wife, not really, not like the way he loved her, and Ruth trembled with rage, at Joanna, at the unfairness, and gazed back at her rival across the dark garden, wishing her dead. She was in pain, it would be a mercy, and then she was shocked at herself for thinking this, because she liked Joanna, had so since they'd met.

At breakfast the next morning Joanna listened as her husband talked, as he smiled and laughed, pretending the conversation of the previous evening hadn't taken place, until she couldn't bear it any longer, putting her hand on his arm, making him stop. 'I meant it, Ralph.'

The desperation he'd felt the night before returned, how could he convince her of the truth, that he loved only her? He covered her hand with his own, his mind calming slightly as a way to resolve the situation came to him. 'I've been thinking, what we need is a more qualified nurse. Ruth has been good enough, but…'

Joanna almost smiled, a new nurse, a new playmate for Ralph, but she had always smiled and put on a brave face; not now though. Even though his indiscretions weren't the reason for her decision, she was glad she would have peace in the time she had left, to have Ralph as a visitor, arriving with his arms full of flowers and a tender kiss, she wouldn't have to know what he did and with whom the rest of the time. 'We'll give Ruth a good reference,' he was saying now, looking towards the dining room door, which led to the passageway to the kitchen where his wife's nurse breakfasted with the other staff.

But Ruth wasn't in the kitchen; she was at the other side of the ajar door, standing there in shock, after overhearing his words on the way past. Her hand was over her mouth to stop herself crying out. She had misheard him, she *must* have.

After breakfast, Joanna waited for Ruth in the bathroom; Ralph read the morning papers in the conservatory while she had her 'bath'. She gazed at the claw-footed tub, remembering the soothing balm of being immersed in water, something she would never experience again... or would she? They'd have a lift—a winch, that was the word she was looking for, where she was going, and she smiled.

There was a knock on the bathroom door and Ruth came in; Joanna noticed that her nurse was pale as she sponged Joanna's neck and arms, she did not seem her usual self. Joanna knew she had led a solitary life before coming here, caring for her elderly parents; she would have had little experience of men, especially flirts like Ralph. Joanna pictured him engrossed in *The Telegraph*, feeling annoyed with him for putting them all in this situation. Ruth had obviously been crying, Joanna saw the puffed redness of her eyes as her nurse dried her skin and refastened her clothes. She hoped the poor girl didn't imagine she was in love with Ralph, and she asked to be taken outside to the summerhouse.

Ruth pushed the wheelchair along the path, having to stop when Joanna wanted to touch and smell pink flowers, naming them; showing me up, thought Ruth, who didn't know the Latin names of any plants. It was Joanna she had realised who wanted rid of her, Joanna who must have insisted they replace her, when she had overheard Ralph say about a reference. Ruth knew he had said it only to pacify Joanna, that he wouldn't be able to bear it any more than she could, for them to be separated.

Once they were inside the summerhouse, she straightened Joanna's rug, tucking it into the sides of the wheelchair, and as Joanna looked up at her, Ruth saw how thin her neck had become, imagined it snapping like a twig under her hands, and her heart raced, but then Joanna touched her arm.

'Sit with me.'

Her voice brought Ruth to her senses, and she sat dazedly, ashamed of her evil thoughts, unable to meet Joanna's eyes, gazing out at the garden instead, seeing Ralph through the French doors of the house, smiling at something he was reading in the paper.

Joanna followed her nurse's gaze. Look at him, she rolled her eyes in irritation, without a care in the world. 'I don't usually come here.' She paused. 'I found my husband here with…' It was humiliating for Joanna, but she must prevent the girl from being hurt if she could, from thinking she was special to Ralph. 'It never lasts long each time.'

After a moment, Ruth stood abruptly, murmuring an excuse to leave, and Joanna watched her retreating figure going up the garden, saw Ralph still absorbed in his paper, and she hated him in that moment as he didn't even notice Ruth in tears, walking up the garden towards the house.

Ralph lowered his paper, looking at his watch, where was Joanna? but then the door opened and he smiled in anticipation of seeing his wife being pushed into the room. Instead, it was Ruth on her own.

Her face was white, her eyes unnaturally bright; he got quickly up. 'Where's Joanna?' Ruth replied that she was in the garden, that she was fine. Relieved, he sat again, reaching for the paper, but had only got through a few lines before realising that Ruth was still standing on the same spot.

'It's not true... she's lying because she's jealous of us, isn't she?'

Ralph gazed back at her with incomprehension.

'I love you... and I know you love me.'

Ralph couldn't believe his ears, almost laughing, catching himself in time.

'Ruth...' he began, but really what was there to say; they'd briefly kissed one night in the summerhouse, that was all, before he restrained himself. It had been a momentary lapse. She wasn't even his type; she'd a good enough figure, but there was a coarseness to her face. 'Actually Ruth, perhaps Joanna mentioned it... I'm afraid we're going to have to let you go. We need someone more experienced.' She didn't reply, just stood like a dummy, staring at him, and he picked up his paper again. When he got to the end of the page he glanced up and she had gone.

In the summerhouse, Joanna adjusted the rug over her knees; the sun didn't reach this end of the garden until later and she felt chilly, but she would have to wait until either Ruth or her husband came. She saw that Ralph was still reading the paper, when he next glanced up she would attract his attention. Then she heard a window being opened, the rub of its wooden frame pushed up, and looked along the house, waving at Ruth who was at an upper storey window.

But Ruth didn't seem to see, and Joanna noticed the blankness of her eyes.

She climbed through the window, sitting on the narrow ledge.

For a moment, Joanna didn't think or do anything, the shock was so great, and then she pushed with all her strength on her wheels, managing to roll from the summerhouse onto the lawn. '*Ruth*,' she called, but the girl didn't look at her, didn't even hear her.

Joanna tried to calm her racing mind, to decide what to do. She looked towards the French doors, willing Ralph to lift his head out of the paper and turn it in her direction, wanting to shout for him, but terrified this might startle Ruth and make her jump.

She pushed again on her wheels, but to no avail on the grass, and now she had no choice but to risk calling Ralph.

He put down the paper, coming through the French doors, she could see him out of the corner of her vision, keeping her gaze on Ruth. She pointed up as he walked across the lawn. 'Good God!' he gasped. '*Ruth?* What, what are you doing?' His head turned towards Joanna, no doubt with a helpless expression, but she couldn't take her eyes from her nurse.

'Ruth, I… I need to talk to you…' Joanna held her breath as they waited for a response. 'You… you were right, I… do love you.'

Joanna watched as Ruth's focus moved in Ralph's direction. 'I need you to wait there, I… I'm coming up. Wait for me, Ruth,' and Joanna whispered, '*Hurry*,' as he disappeared through the French doors, and then it seemed an interminable time before Ruth's head turned towards the inside of the room, and finally she climbed back through the window out of sight.

Later, Joanna gazed at the telephone on the hall table, her resolution wavering. Despite the events of the morning, despite his many faults, she couldn't bear the thought of being separated from him. Maybe it *was* too soon, she reasoned, it might be years after all before she was bedridden, as Ralph had pointed out. And although she was angry with him at the moment, she still loved him, and believed in his love for her, and only her, despite Ruth, and the ones before. She knew other people wouldn't understand how that could be, they would think her a fool, hearing again Ralph calling up to Ruth at the window earlier, telling her nurse...

'I do love you,' the words repeated again in Ruth's mind as she lay on her bed, waiting. And to think she had almost, still would, if... but he had declared his love, calling to her at the window for the world to hear, for Joanna to hear, and now there would be no more pretence, they could both look after Joanna until... and then they would finally be together, she just, *they* just, had to be patient; and she sighed with contentment, listening for his tread on the stairs, he'd said that he would check on her later...

Ralph was also listening, stilled in the conservatory, his pen poised above a sheet of paper; it had sounded like someone clearing their throat, and he went over, opening the door. Joanna's wheelchair was beside the hall table. 'Darling, are you warm enough?'

'I'm fine,' she replied, without turning her head. He went to speak again, but changed his mind, closing the door softly instead.

He picked up his pen again, the sharpness of *I'm fine*, wounded him, but then what else could be expected after the debacle of earlier. He reread his first sentence: *Ruth was hard-working and dedicated to her patient, although had a tendency to become over emotional.* He wasn't sure whether this was appropriate, but better to be honest, he decided, wishing someone had warned *him* that Ruth would mistake flattering words for something entirely different.

She needed a new position quickly, he reminded himself, remembering with acute anxiety that this business had almost made Joanna leave him, and he crumpled up the sheet of paper, starting again: *Ruth was hard-working and dedicated to her patient, and had a pleasant and friendly nature.* They would have to be extremely careful when choosing Joanna's new nurse; in fact—the solution came to Ralph—maybe they should get a male nurse, no more of these silly girls with their infatuations, making a nuisance of themselves. But then he thought of this male nurse washing Joanna… an older woman instead, approaching retirement age, yes, that would be best, and he couldn't wait to tell Joanna that he had everything solved. He heard the murmur of her voice in the hall, as though talking on the telephone, and he quickly finished Ruth's reference.

'Until next week then.' Joanna replaced the receiver, realising she was smiling, not apprehensive as expected about the dramatic change about to happen in her life. It had been her decision, hers alone; she might no longer be able to move her legs, but her mind was still clear and capable. There had been a deterioration lately in her condition that she could no longer ignore, which made sitting even more painful, and she knew she had to face the reality that it would probably be months, not years, until she would no longer have a use for her wheelchair.

She could hear Ralph's footsteps approaching. 'Darling, come in to the fire, it's cold out here.' Then he said something about writing a reference for Ruth, and she almost replied *Whom you love*—even though she knew he didn't—to see him suffer, to hear him protest again that he had no choice, to keep her from... 'We'll employ a more experienced nurse this time,' he went on, and as he spoke, movement caught Joanna's eye, and she turned her head, seeing Ruth on the staircase, a hand raised to her mouth, in shock at his words.

Look at her, thought Joanna. She loves him, same as I do. We're a pair of fools. Suddenly she was angry, at herself, at Ralph, even annoyed at Ruth for being taken in by him. Leave him—wasn't that what everyone had told her over the years, had said he didn't deserve her, that she *couldn't* still love him.

'I've been telephoning the residential home I told you about,' she said, 'a lovely place where...'

'No!' A cry from her husband, in contrast to the hope and almost joy Joanna could see on her nurse's face.

'My mind is made up.'

'This is ridiculous! Tell her Ruth, tell her there is

nothing between us!'

Ruth stared intently at Joanna.

If he has broken his promise, I won't allow him to visit me, thought Joanna. I warned him it was his last chance. It will be difficult to bear, but I have to have *some* dignity, *some* self-respect.

Ruth looked from her to Ralph.

'Tell her,' Ralph was distraught, imploring with his hands.

Ruth's father had been a vicar, remembered Joanna. She had seen her reading her bible. Telling the truth would be important to her.

'In the summerhouse,' Ruth finally spoke. 'I know it was a sin… but we are in love.'

Vermin

The intensity of her grief will pass. She knows this; she should do at her age, but it doesn't make it easier.

Philip isn't grieving, not even pretending. You would think for her sake, when it's obvious how upset she is, he would express *some* sense of loss. His lack of sorrow hurts her, but what else did she expect? She knows he had never liked Maisie May, right from their first meeting.

It had been foolishness on her part, to think that he would grow to love her, that the fuss he made would only be temporary, when he came home from work one evening and saw the new arrival in her arms, a tiny whisp of ginger fluff.

She explained she'd found the poor little mite shivering under a bush in the park, how it had taken ages to coax her out.

'It's just with my asthma,' he had said. 'If it wasn't for that…'

Then a big deal was made of everything, even something simple like a cat flap, saying that mice would get in, could she not let the cat out the door instead.

The cat.

They had met when he joined her reading club at the library; she had thought him a kind, thoughtful man, a companion for her later years, but she began to see a different side to him. He hadn't gone with her to the vets for Maisie May's inoculations, or to the pet store for all the things she needed, didn't admire the gorgeous pink velvet collar with the cutest little bell.

Instead, he tried to make out that his chest was worse. He even went to the doctor; cat hair would aggravate it he was supposedly told, even more so than that of a dog.

She hoovered the house more often so he had no excuse to complain, was already hoovering as he left for work, again after dinner, again as he watched the ten o'clock news. He started walking, every night, even in the rain, even in the cold. No wonder he had a bad chest.

Now Maisie May is gone, he sits in front of the TV again, never venturing out in the evening, even though it is summertime, even though it is perfect walking weather.

'There's kittens advertised in the paper,' she says, and knows immediately from his expression that she was right to suspect him. 'One might be lonely separated from the rest. I think I'll get two.'

He puts his hand inside his jacket pocket where he keeps his inhaler, as if the very thought of two cats in the house will give him an asthma attack. The only way he could redeem himself now would be to say: *But it's too soon after Maisie May.* If he was clever, he would say that, pretending he had liked her. But he isn't clever; he has only been promoted once in his thirty-two years with Prentice Printers.

'It's just with my...'

'You're right, it's not a good idea,' she replies, even giving him a sympathetic smile. 'And we'll be able to go on holiday now,' she adds, just to see his reaction.

As expected, his face lights up.

The summer before Maisie May arrived, they'd gone to Blackpool. He had wanted to put her in a cattery so they could go to Cornwall the following year.

A cattery.

She goes for a walk, unable to bear being in the house with him, never mind go on holiday. Her fingers fiddle with the collar in her pocket, listening to the muffled chime of the tiny bell. It was still impossible to believe someone had wanted to deliberately harm Maisie May.

'Poisoning.' She'll never forget the vet saying it.

'There's ethylene glycol… anti-freeze,' he had continued, 'in the stomach contents.'

'Wh-what do you mean?' She had struggled to get the words out.

'It has a very sweet taste, cats like it.'

'You… you mean… someone *on purpose?*'

'Not everyone's a cat lover I'm afraid.'

That evening, she had told Philip everything the vet said, intently watching his face for signs of guilt.

'Maybe he means pigeon keepers,' he finally replied.

She had stared at him with incomprehension.

'When the vet said not everyone's a cat lover. It's common knowledge that pigeon keepers hate cats.'

She has walked further than intended, and has already been up and down this road several times before, looking for a pigeon shed in someone's garden, for any sign of birds.

Her fingers clasp tighter to the collar in her pocket. There are no pigeon keepers; she has been around the whole area.

No one else had wanted rid of her.

She feels overcome at the realisation that it *must* have been Philip, putting out a hand to steady herself, holding onto the garden fence beside her. How easy it must have been, to take the anti-freeze from the garage shelf, to pour it into a saucer.

'Can I help you?'

A man walks down the driveway towards her; he must think she's loitering outside his house.

She pulls herself together, letting go of the fence.

'You okay?'

He's young; half her age. She isn't used to being treated courteously by the younger generation, more used to being pushed past in the supermarket, ignored by them in queues.

She smiles at him. 'I'm fine, thank you.' As she begins to walk away, she pauses, turning back. 'Actually, I wonder if you could tell me… are there any pigeon keepers around here?'

He looks at her strangely; she knows it was an odd question to ask. 'Why?' he says. 'Why d'you want to know?'

She flounders for a moment. 'It's just… I like them. I like pigeons.'

He shakes his head. 'None round here, far as I know.'

She walks on, berating herself for saying *I like them*. Pigeon keepers liked pigeons, people who were capable of poisoning other people's beloved cats. People like her husband.

The first time she does it, it's unintentional. Philip

takes tablets each morning. They are already in a box with compartments for each day of the week, and she tips them into an egg cup. But today she accidentally spills them onto the bench, because she's upset, anyone in her situation would be, not concentrating on what she is doing. She scoops them up and puts them into the egg cup, four tablets... no, wait, there's just three. She looks on the bench, on the floor, to no avail... She waits for him to notice at breakfast that one isn't there, but he tips them into his mouth and washes them down with tea as usual.

He comes home that evening with a travel guide to Cornwall, saying that he slipped out to get it in his lunch break.

'Did you have a good day? How was your chest?' she asks.

He smiles, yes, his day was fine and so was he, clearly pleased that she cares about his wellbeing.

Again, the second time, it's not intentional, not really. She is looking at the vitamin tablets she got a while back and never took. They're very similar, she thinks, to one of Philip's four. She swops them over in the egg cup, you really couldn't tell the difference, and then Philip is behind her, carrying the tray with the breakfast things over to the table, before she can swap them back.

There wouldn't have been a third time, if he hadn't done it. Maisie May's basket was gone from the corner of the kitchen. It had been there the previous night; she always looked at it before going up to bed, blinking back a tear, picturing her darling curled up inside. She found it in the garage, beside the bin, and she knew he'd almost put it *in* the bin, then thought better of it.

She doesn't mean to continue, but can't seem to stop herself, keeps picturing him filling a saucer in the garage, watching it being lapped up. And anyway, he mustn't need them, his health issues are obviously exaggerated to get sympathy—Poor Philip and his bad chest.

The phone call one day surprises her, from her husband's office, to say he has been taken to hospital with heart palpitations after a severe asthma attack.

He looks pale and drained at visiting time and she berates herself; how could she have done it? He has to take off his oxygen mask to speak to her, telling her not to worry; then puts it back over his mouth, closing his eyes as if it was such an effort to talk.

The following day the hospital contacts her. Her heart flutters, what if they've realised he wasn't on his proper medication? They are ringing to tell her that he has picked up a viral infection. 'But he has a weak chest!' she replies, panic rising in her voice, and they say that visitors aren't allowed into his ward at the moment to limit the spread of infection.

As soon as she sets down the phone, it rings again.

When she finds out who is calling, she has to reach out a hand to steady herself, gripping the back of a kitchen chair. But she is being ridiculous, she tells herself, he's hardly going to accuse her of making Philip ill!

'I believe your cat was poisoned,' the policeman says.

'Y-yes.' She can barely speak.

He explains that he's been contacted by her vet.

'There have been similar incidents in your area,' the policeman continues. 'We're following a line of enquiry.'

She goes outside after the call, trying to clear her mind, walking blindly along the road. *If not Philip, then...* A van toots, and she realises she has stepped off the pavement. *How could she have?* It's only an infection, she reminds herself, people must pick them up all the time in hospital. *But with his bad chest...*

She walks faster, trying not to think... faster still, chasing away thoughts... but now she's out of breath, dizzy even, and must stop; there's a fence beside her, the same one she held last time. She tries to compose herself...

It's then that she hears it, but it must be her mind playing tricks, because that was what she was listening for last time she walked this far—cooing.

There it is again, and she walks slowly forward, up the driveway and along the side of the house; it's as though the birds are calling her. There's a large shed, and she can smell them now, the way a cat would, drawing it in.

'Can I help you?' A young woman has appeared with a toddler on her hip, wary of this stranger in her back yard.

She has to think quickly. 'Your husband. I... I was talking to your husband.' She indicates to the shed. 'I... like them... pigeons that is.'

The woman smiles. 'They only come this week.'

She forms her mouth into a return smile. *'Really?'*

The woman shifts the toddler onto her other hip. 'We moved in a month back, but Gary didn't want to bring them til now. You got any?'

She shakes her head. 'No… no, there's too many cats where I live.'

The woman nods. 'I like cats, me, but some chance us gettin one.' Her gaze moves to the shed. 'Gary says they're vermin.'

She doesn't remember the walk back home.

She had liked him, that day at his house, for asking if she was okay. *Gary says they're vermin.*

It's not intentional; it's not as if she purposely waits until dark; it's not as if she plans it. She lies in bed with the curtains open, thinking—*It's a bright night, the moon will light the way.* She gets up, gets dressed, goes downstairs. Carries what she needs.

The birds are startled, kick up a racket, so she has to be quick before Gary appears; he's probably already jumping out of bed, thinking, *Bet it's another bastard cat.* She waits only until she's sure it's properly caught, and the flames are racing up towards the moon. The birds are shrieking now, screaming for Gary to save them as she walks back down the driveway.

When she gets home, she sits at the kitchen table until daylight, and then she packs Philip's underwear and another pair of pyjamas to leave at the hospital. She wonders if Gary is there, his hands and arms burnt—she feels regret for a moment, but then pictures him pouring the anti-freeze, and her remorse shrivels away.

The Cornwall brochure is in the magazine rack; she puts it into the bag with the pyjamas. This will make it up to Philip.

The telephone rings.

She stares at it, her mind racing; *What if it's the hospital, what if...* the ringing seems to grow louder, accusing her.

Eventually, it stops.

'Pull yourself together,' she says out loud. 'They will have been phoning to say he's on the mend, that he can have visitors... Yes, of course that will be it! He'll be so pleased to see me.'

As she puts on her coat the doorbell buzzes; through the hall window she can see the bright blue and yellow lines of a police car. She sighs deeply, it really isn't a good time... but it shouldn't take long, and then she can be on her way to the hospital.

Through the front door's frosted glass a pair of uniformed silhouettes are visible at the other side. She straightens her shoulders, ready to explain about last night, to answer questions; she can even show them the paraffin canister and matches in the garage where she left them.

'Vermin,' she will say. 'I was just getting rid of vermin.'

The Message

It hadn't shocked him when it arrived.

He pictured someone else in his situation, the blood draining from their face, a hand on their heart.

FATHER O'MALLEY neatly written across the envelope.

There wasn't a note inside, no words of threat or intent, but then there wasn't a need. The message was clear from its content—a bullet in the post.

In a strange way he was almost glad it came; it meant the days of his indecision were over. He knew what he had to do.

There was a rapping on his door, and he limped across the room with the envelope, putting it away in a drawer.

'Come in!'

Father O'Malley had been expecting Reverend Crosby to pay him a visit, since the news broke of what had happened, since the shadow of the past darkened their lives again.

A shaking of hands, the firmness of the other man's grasp, a reminder to the priest of their first meeting those years ago, the strong grip he had thought then, perhaps a mark of the man's character, and so it had proved.

'It has begun again,' said the Reverend, always one to get to the point.

Father O'Malley nodded.

'An innocent man on his way to work.'

Another solemn nod.

'Will we take it to the Lord in prayer?'

Reverend Crosby invariably used these same words.

He had used them the first time he had come to see the priest, the day after the chapel was set on fire. 'Not in my name, or any decent Protestant in this town.' The Reverend had been indignant, his colour high. Had anyone seen him at my door? was all the priest could think, knowing there would be trouble if they had. 'Will we take it to the Lord in prayer?' Reverend Crosby had continued. Father O'Malley had been shocked. The Reverend had seen his shock; 'Is it not the same God we both love?' he had said. 'I'll begin… Lord in Heaven, we come to you today with troubled hearts. With grief in our hearts for the members of our community who have committed this despicable act. We pray that there will be no retaliation…'

Troubled times that had been past, but were here again, Father O'Malley thought now. He had watched the funeral on the news. This latest incident had left another bereft family, had destroyed the ceasefire.

The two men prayed, Reverend Crosby starting, and Father O'Malley continuing, as was their custom. There had been repercussions, as the priest had assumed after their first meeting, a quiet word from the Bishop prompted by concerned parishioners, and the Reverend's superior no doubt had something to say about it.

But they had continued to meet, just a few times a year, to pray, to reflect on how the two sides of their community could live peacefully without this bloodshed. And their prayers had been answered.

The chapel and the Presbyterian church were only a stone's throw apart. Father O'Malley smiled to himself at the irony of his thinking this cliché—as well as being petrol-bombed, the chapel windows had been stoned; the black stone exterior regularly de-faced by paint. Reverend Crosby was always the first to offer sympathy, to insist that the perpetrators were not approved of by him, as if Father O'Malley didn't know about the Loyalist gangs, about the grip they had on this small town, as if he thought the Reverend in any way responsible.

Now, the Reverend shook the priest's hand again before taking his leave, and Father O'Malley knew what his reaction would be, if he told him about what came today in the post. He wouldn't understand why the priest had not gone straightaway to the police.

He had taken Reverend Crosby inside the chapel at their first meeting, to show him the damage caused by the fire. The Reverend had gazed at the confessional, intrigued. 'The things you must have heard.' He had said this almost to himself, but the priest had always had good hearing, still did despite his age. The things I wish I hadn't heard, he had thought afterwards.

'Bless me Father, for I have sinned.' And he had blessed, had forgiven, had absolved each and every time. *In persona Christi*; he had never forgotten that he was only the vessel, that the confession was to God, the absolution also from Him.

'I… took another man's life, Father.' Even then the priest had not faltered, and at least there had been anguish, heart-felt remorse, in the voice at the other side of the grille.

'You must give yourself up, my child.'

The priest had prayed for him, what seemed like a continual prayer day and night, awake and asleep, 'Hear me in the name of Jesus your beloved Son, for the sake of this young man, for the others tempted along his path.'

And there had been others like him, saying those same words, and the priest had never wavered in his reply.

'Are you all right, Father?' the Reverend asked him now, as they shook hands.

I have never been inside *his* church, thought the priest. *I* would never have made the first contact, knocked on his door, extended the hand of friendship.

Love thy neighbour: the second greatest commandment. Hadn't he told the Bishop that they ought to set the example of tolerance, of peace. He had only stopped himself in time from adding, Do we both not love the same God?

Father O'Malley gripped the minister's hand tighter. 'Bless you. Bless you, Reverend Crosby.'

Alone again, the priest went to the drawer, taking out the envelope. He sat at his table, tipping the content into his hand. *You must go immediately to the police,* Reverend Crosby would have said, the colour rising in his cheeks, the way it did when his emotions were running high. But he hadn't told him, hadn't shown him this terrible thing in his hand.

'I killed a man, Father.'

Just a few days ago, this was spoken through the grille. There was a lack of emotion, of remorse in the voice. But the priest knew how he must respond. Forgiveness, of course he had to pass on God's forgiveness. But, he reasoned with himself, there *also* had to be a suitable penance, as well as repentant prayers for a mortal sin. How else would this stop, these terrible crimes that had started again.

'My child, you must give yourself up.' Then the priest heard himself add, 'If you don't, I shall.'

'After which I will be excommunicated,' he said out loud now. He looked again at the bullet in his hand. 'Or perhaps there won't be a need for that.'

The priest's encouragement to give oneself up had not been followed through in the past. But he had to insist on it this time; these killings could not be allowed to begin again. To be carried out by a new generation, by a young man, just seventeen or eighteen. His family was well known to the priest; they were regular attendees to Mass. He had been a chorister as a child, the priest recalled, remembering his beautiful singing voice.

'I killed a man, Father.'

Then, receiving the sacrament of the bread and wine. *'This is my body…'* he had lowered his head, opening his mouth; his lower lip was discoloured, the priest noticed. *'This is the chalice of my blood…'* he had looked up then at Father O'Malley and there was no contrition in his eyes, as there had been none in his confession.

Father O'Malley returned the envelope to the drawer, put on his coat, his hat and gloves. He only had an hour before he had to be back for Mass. He knew his place of work, perhaps he could catch him on his lunch break.

As he turned the street corner of the factory, he saw him at the gates.

'Hello, Sean.'

He didn't make eye contact with the priest. 'Father.'

In the silence that followed, he put his hands in his overall pockets, scuffing the heel of his boot on the pavement. He looks even younger than his years, thought the priest, trying to picture this innocent-looking boy writing his name on the envelope, putting the bullet inside.

'Sean…' the priest began, and he raised his head. The coldness of his gaze, the blankness of it, almost made Father O'Malley take an involuntary step back, as now he could imagine him with the envelope, could even picture him with a gun in his hand. A drive-by shooting, it had said on the news. A Protestant man on his way to work, ground down on his way to work.

'If you don't,' the priest held Sean's gaze, 'I shall.'

The same words that he had said in the confessional, ones he had hoped he wouldn't have to follow through.

The boy's eyes stayed with the priest, stayed with him during Mass; stayed with him as he sat again at his table, facing the drawer, with the envelope inside. He rubbed his bad knee, thinking how his excommunication would cause a stir, but just for a short time. He would be quickly replaced, and in a few years the parish would barely remember him; they would choose to forget the betrayer, one of their own, but no longer so.

He would miss his visits from Reverend Crosby. He should be thinking instead about his own parishioners, his fellow priests, the Bishop, but it was the Presbyterian minister who had first come to mind.

The priest sat for a moment longer, then got up, putting on his coat, his hat and gloves, dressed for a journey, forgetting that he would only be crossing the road. I'll be seen; I'll be reported, he thought, as he reached the steps up to the Presbyterian church.

He went to open the front door, but hesitated; what if this was their time of... he had almost thought 'Mass'.

He hadn't known what to expect inside, but it wasn't this, the similarity to the sacred atmosphere of the chapel. Of course, there were differences too; no kneelers in the pews he noticed, walking slowly up the central aisle. No confessional.

In the corner, beside the pulpit, was a glass fronted cabinet with a silver jug and plate inside—Communion vessels—and he remembered that they believed the bread and wine mere symbols of Christ's body and blood, not his Real Presence, and the gulf, the great divide between the faiths opened before him, just as the two sides of the town's community stood either side of an unbridgeable chasm.

'Father O'Malley?' The Reverend's anxious voice behind him. 'Has something else happened?'

The priest turned around. 'No, everything's fine. I... just thought I'd pay you a visit,' realising as he said it that the Reverend had visited *him* that very morning.

The Reverend smiled, a glint of amusement in his eyes, no doubt having the same thought. 'I was just about to put the kettle on…' already leading the way, and the priest followed him past the pulpit to a door at the back of the church, crossing the imaginary chasm he had seen opening before him, ashamed now of his thinking it.

Later, as he sat again at his own table, the priest wondered if he had been seen. The Bishop's quiet word in Father O'Malley's ear over the years about the Reverend coming to his door, would be different in tone and content, if he learned that the priest had crossed the road, and entered the Protestant church in broad daylight.

It would be an inconsequential matter though, compared with his informing on one of their own, and he would be paying a visit to the police station, of that he was now sure, the boy would not go of his own volition.

Then, he would have to leave the priesthood. His faith and his calling—that was the sum of what had been. Then it would just be his faith. He smiled to himself at his thinking the word *just*, when it was all he needed, all he *would* need, to remain in the grace of God.

He was still smiling as he knelt to pray, but as he closed his eyes there was a noise outside. He stilled, listening, glancing at the clock on the wall. It wasn't yet nine o'clock; his custom was to lock the door before retiring to bed at ten.

The sound, whatever it was, wasn't repeated, but all

the same, perhaps he should turn the key now. He struggled up, going over to the door. It opened abruptly as he reached it, flinging open in fact, almost knocking him down.

The hooded man shut the door behind him, indicating with the gun in his hand for Father O'Malley to step back, away from him.

'You'll not mind if I sit down, Sean,' said the priest. 'My knee's giving me a spot of bother.' He drew back a chair at the table.

A balaclava covered the boy's face, with holes for his eyes and mouth, revealing the faded bruise on his lower lip. He was breathing heavily, the priest also noticed, indicating his nervousness. The gun though was steady in his hand, his eyes devoid of expression.

The priest rubbed his sore knee, panicking the boy, who shook the gun at him to put his hands back up where he could see them.

'What age are you, Sean?' The priest asked the question rhetorically, knowing he wasn't going to speak. 'Seventeen? Eighteen?'

The gun was aimed at his head now, the boy's hand steady again. Just the raggedness of his breathing revealed his emotion.

'I was in a gang when I was your age.'

There was a flash of shock in the boy's eyes, and the priest realised that making this revelation was an admittance to himself that his life on earth would most likely end tonight. He had never spoken of this part of his history to anyone before now.

'I see that has surprised you, Sean. Not that it was

called a gang in those days. *A bad lot*, that was how they were described. They wanted me; I don't know why me especially. I was a quiet boy, perhaps because I was tall and strong. They wanted me for the cause.

'You'll know all about the cause, Sean, they'll have drummed it into you, like they did to me. I didn't know I had an enemy until they told me about them—the people I passed every day in the street.'

The boy moved closer, holding the weapon with both hands now, and the priest knew he wanted it over with.

'I was frightened Sean, like you are now. Frightened of being one of them. Frightened of what would happen if I wasn't.' He pointed at his knee. 'This was for not obeying an order.'

The boy's eyes moved, as if he was considering the priest's words, but it was only momentary, before the blankness returned.

'Walk away now, Sean. In the name of God, walk away child while you still can.'

The boy moved closer still, taking aim, and the priest began to pray.

A knock sounded on the door.

The priest held up a hand. They'd go away again, whoever it was, in a moment, but it had spooked the boy, as he moved back, so he wouldn't be seen if the door opened.

Another knock.

An intense pain spread across the priest's chest.

The door opened.

'Ah, you are here, Father.' Reverend Crosby held

gloves in his hand. 'You left these behind…'

The Reverend stepped into the room; the priest shook his head, his chest constricting until he could scarcely breathe. 'Are you all right, Father?'

The door closed, and the Reverend turned around, seeing the boy, seeing the gun in his hands.

'This is between us,' the priest struggled to speak. 'Let him leave.'

Strength of character, hadn't the priest always thought that of the Reverend, but now he wished it wasn't so, as the minister walked without hesitation across the room to stand beside him, and Father O'Malley began to pray again, no longer for himself, but for the man by his side.

'No harm has been done,' the Reverend reached out his hands towards the boy, beseeching him to put down the gun. 'This can be resolved. Whatever this is about, can be resolved.'

The weapon didn't waver in the boy's outstretched hands.

The Reverend took a step towards him, still speaking, and the priest moved faster than he had thought himself capable, and in the fleeting second before he went down, he thanked God that his knee hadn't seized, thanked God that he would be the one.

As Father O'Malley had predicted, it did cause a stir in the parish, in the entire town, when he was replaced. The new priest, encouraged by the Bishop, tried to draw a line under the newspaper headlines, and the rumours circling the chapel—*Bullet in the post from Loyalist scum… Retaliation for drive-by shooting…*

A new door with a peep hole had replaced Father O'Malley's old one. It was kept locked, with any visitors being allowed through only at the priest's discretion. A rap now, on the door just before dark, was a cause for concern for the new priest, especially with emotions running so high in the town, and when he saw who his visitor was, he kept still and silent, waiting for him to go away.

Another rap, louder this time, and the new priest watched with consternation as the handle moved down on his side of the locked door. The Bishop had made his view of any contact between the chapel and the Protestant church across the road clear, and the new priest, just a young man, knew to follow orders.

Footsteps sounded walking away, and he breathed more easily. *Died in the arms of…* Of all the rumours surrounding O'Malley's death, this seemed the most fanciful to the young priest, but he didn't dwell; he was taking his first Mass in the morning and needed to prepare.

He would hear his first confession. The thought of being behind the grille *in persona Christi,* filled him with anxiety for a moment, before he pulled himself together.

Just like Father O'Malley and all of the priests before him, he would know how to react to, how to respond to, anything he heard in the confessional.

Of course he would.

Lilies

My mother is my only visitor each month. She fiddles with her handbag strap, asking how I am. I look pale, have I not been well? Usually, she does all of the talking, but today I have something to ask her. I want her to put flowers on Gail's grave.

Lilies were her favourite. On our wedding day their intense, heavy perfume filled the church. I waited at the altar, trying to keep still, clasping, unclasping my hands, and then she was there. I stilled, watching her walk towards me, smiling, her face overflowing with happiness, a reflection of mine.

What will I ask my mother to buy? All I can think of are wreaths of flowers, as it will also be the anniversary of Gail's death. I try only to remember our wedding day, but there it is again in my head, I can't stop it, the sequence of noise—the first thump of her body hitting the stairs, then repeating in succession as she gained momentum down them. The terrible crack of her head hitting the hall tiles, the worst sound.

My mother has run out of things to say. It is the same each visit. She must plan things to talk about, to keep me in touch with the outside world. When these peter-out we fall into silence. She looks distressed, glancing around the room. I wish I could spare her coming here, say there's no need, but I can't bring myself to utter the words, because she is all I have.

I have told her, in the same way I had to tell the police, all about my marriage. She said that she believed me, but her expression said otherwise. I didn't blame her; if the police didn't believe me then why should she?

It started on an ordinary day. I got home from work, and Gail came in soon after. We had only been married two months. I couldn't concentrate at work; all I could think of was Gail.

'There's a new restaurant opening,' I began. 'Apparently it...'

'Did you get milk?' she interrupted.

I shook my head. 'I forgot.'

It must only have taken seconds, but I can see it now in slow motion—her hand rising, slapping me across the face. She turned, picked up her handbag, walking out the door. The rev of her car started up in the driveway.

When she came back, she set the milk carton on the bench. 'What would you like for dinner, Paul? Let's ring for a takeaway. Chinese or Indian? You decide, darling.'

I forgot about it afterwards. Gail and I decorated the house at the weekends. We even did some gardening, although neither of us knew a flower from a weed. Her parents called in unexpectedly and found me chasing her around the lawn with the hose, both of us soaked, squealing and laughing like children.

That evening, I assembled a coffee table we had ordered. One of the legs wouldn't fit in, and I hunkered, drilling the hole bigger. Gail said something behind me, but I couldn't hear her above the noise of the drill, and then she bumped into me on her way past.

She turned back when I cried out, her voice irritated,

'What have you done?' On the drive to A&E she was concerned, 'You'll have to be more careful, Paul.'

For our first wedding anniversary I planned a surprise weekend, to the hotel in Devon where we'd spent our honeymoon. Gail unpacked the top layer of the suitcase. 'Remember that waiter.' I laughed. 'The one who brought us breakfast and we…'

'Where's the camera, Paul?' She tossed our clothes out of the case, onto the bed. 'You said you'd put it in.'

'We can get a disposable.'

The wooden hanger in her hand caught me in the stomach. I stumbled backwards, trying to catch my breath. She looked at me, her eyes vacant, as though she didn't know me. 'I'll finish unpacking while you go and buy one.'

It became a joke at the office—my clumsiness at DIY. 'Do you want me to give you a hand,' Ben offered, 'before you do yourself serious harm?'

'No!' I'd said it too sharply. 'You'd best not risk it.' I laughed.

I couldn't always work out what I had done, or forgotten to do. I jotted things down in a notebook— what Gail had said that day, what I had said. I didn't have to remember to tell her I loved her. I did that every night, before we went to sleep.

I got to know the warning signs—the abruptness of her movements, the dark flush of her skin. If I moved quickly, I could sometimes get out of the room in time.

'Did they not shout a warning?' my boss wanted to know.

His face blurred. 'Sorry, what did you say?'

'It's a wonder you weren't knocked out…'

I woke up in a cubicle; voices sounded on the other side of the curtain. My shirt was unbuttoned; I hurriedly closed it, tearing off one of the buttons in my rush. Something covered my right temple. When I touched it, the throbbing intensified.

'It'll be sore for a while.' A nurse had appeared. 'Hit by a golf ball your colleague said?'

I nodded, tried to smile.

'We got ceramic shards out of the wound, like from a cup or plate.'

She waited for me to reply.

'You need to be driven home. Will I call someone for you?'

A sudden, overwhelming need rushed through me. 'Mum…' my voice was choking, 'c-could you ring my mother?'

She fussed as we drove. I didn't speak, letting her concerned voice soak through me. At home she made me strong, sweet tea.

'I didn't even know you played golf.'

She sat opposite me at the kitchen table. I began telling her how I'd only just taken it up…

'Paul?'

My eyes filled. The words somehow came out. 'It—was—Gail.'

I tried to explain, 'She got a promotion at work. We went out to celebrate.'

The evening had started well, Gail was happy, laughing and flirting with the waiter. When we got home, she wanted coffee. I should have made it for her.

She opened a cupboard door, taking out a mug, turning quickly around.

'It was my fault.'

'You must be concussed, dear. You're not making any sense.'

'Did Dad… ever… hit you?'

I stretched my hands across the table, putting them over hers. I couldn't see her face through my tears. The relief of telling her was overwhelming.

She reached me tissues, and I realised her eyes were cold now as she gazed at me. 'It's not my place to interfere in your marriage, Paul, but I'll just say this. A man should never raise his hand to a woman. Don't look for sympathy from me because Gail has hit you back.'

On our second anniversary I bought Gail a watch. I couldn't steady my fingers to wrap it. She smiled when she opened it, hugging me, 'Thank you, darling.' I smiled too; breathed again. She told me over dinner in her favourite restaurant that she wanted us to have a baby.

I wanted one too. Of course, I wanted us to have a family, but I didn't say it quickly enough. I talked too much then, making plans—the spare room could become a nursery; I could make a cot; what names did she like? She didn't reply, silently drinking the rest of the wine. My babbling ran out.

She went upstairs when we got home. I made her coffee; waited, made a fresh cup; waited. Then, I finally went up. She was asleep, sprawled across the bed, still fully dressed.

I went back out onto the landing, opening the spare room door. We could paint it lemon, I had suggested in my overbright voice in the restaurant, that would suit a boy or a girl.

'You don't want a baby.' She was behind me. I turned around. She said it again, shouted it, moving closer. I grabbed her wrist before her fist reached my face. Her eyes were shocked; I was shocked. I tightened my grip and she screamed, trying to fight me off, but I had her other arm now, pushing her against the wall.

She stopped struggling, her body limp and heavy against mine; I came to my senses, 'I'm sorry.' I hugged her to me, my mouth pressed into her hair, 'I'm so sorry. I love you.' I tried to keep hold of her, but she broke away. As she reached the staircase her head turned back, screaming at me to keep away from her.

'Gail!' But she had already stumbled.

The police preferred their version: *Okay, so you and your wife fought, what's new? You slap her around… Okay, so she started slapping you back. One night she goes too far. You're at the top of the stairs. You've had enough…*

The visit is almost over. I still haven't asked my mother about the flowers. She buttons her coat slowly, not wanting to seem anxious to leave, to get out into the fresh air. It must be exhausting for her—the drive here, the strained conversation. I shouldn't burden her with marking my anniversary, but there is no one else to ask.

'Could… would you… get me flowers… for Saturday?' I look down at the table, anywhere, but at her. 'Lilies… I would like lilies for Gail.'

She doesn't respond. I can feel her eyes on me.

I raise my head. She gazes back at me, her face intent. Her memory will be the same as mine—Gail's beautiful smile, her hands full of lilies, trailing down her wedding dress.

I wait for her to reply, but she seems lost in thought.

Finally, she speaks. 'Pollen came off a lily and stained Gail's dress… We got it sponged off, just a small mark was left, but she was angry. I put it down to bridal nerves. Her anger flared up and then just as quickly disappeared and she was smiling again.'

She gazes at me, still and intense… I'm afraid to blink, for the moment to pass.

'You still love her…' her voice wavers.

I nod, unable to speak.

'You couldn't hurt her… She flared up like that with you, didn't she? She… she hurt you.'

I nod again. My voice has deserted me.

She stretches her hands across the table, putting them on mine, trying to speak through her tears. She has let me down, how could she have thought…

She opens her bag, bringing out a hanky to wipe her eyes. 'You have to forget her now.'

The bell goes; visiting time is over.

'Lilies…' I implore her with my eyes.

She sighs heavily, then slowly nods.

I smile.

Lilies for my beautiful bride.

Unravelling

The gate is open.

Clara's hand flies to her mouth.

But he'll still be here! He'll be asleep on the back doorstep, it's a sun trap this time of the day. She hurries along the path, Drew will never forgive her, please let him be here…

She can see the step now…

Into the house, then searching the garden. 'Baxter!' A short pause. *'Baxter!'*

Back down to the gate. She'd been late for work, rushing…

Onto the road, *'Baxter!'*

Getting into the car again, driving, eyes peeled… stopping. 'Excuse me? Have you seen a golden Labrador? Excuse me?' Putting her head into her hands.

Pull yourself together, Clara. Think…

Kim's! He knows his way there. She starts to drive again; he loved those treats she got him last time, Clara smiling and shaking her head. 'You spoil him, same as Drew…' she glances at her watch, in just a few hours her husband will be back from work.

Scanning the road… *Baxter, where are you?* He'll be at Kim's, she tells herself again, the number of times they've walked there, he could do it in his sleep. She has started working from home; she'll see him through the study window.

Turning into her street, *please let him be here*, turning

into her driveway. Oh…

Drew's car is parked beside Kim's.

Why would he be…

She gets out of the car… study window, empty chair at desk… round to the back door, into the kitchen, no Baxter… no Kim or Drew.

Into the hall. She hears something…

Walks across the hall towards the snug.

Hears it again.

Stops.

She recognises it now, the sound, the moan he makes when he's close to… the door is ajar; she takes another step, hears his voice. 'That's it…' The sound of laboured breathing. 'Oh, that's so good.'

Outside again, driving, don't think… tooting, she has veered across the road, just get home… don't think… home… home.

Through the open gate. Along the path towards the back door…

Baxter?

Baxter is lying on the step.

Into the house. She sits on the sofa, gazing blankly ahead at the fireplace. Kim… Kim and Drew… her sister and Drew.

She tries to sort it out in her head…

Her gaze moves to the sideboard, to one of the frames, 50-50-50 around the edges, Kim's present to him last month at the party, his photograph in it, blowing out the candles; Kim's dress sleeve is visible, she'd been sitting next to him… his leg could have been pressed against hers under the table…

Something touches her hand, startling her... it's just Baxter's nose. She gazes at him. 'I don't... how could?'

He lies down at her feet.

She has to sort it out in her head before he comes home.

She stares at the fireplace.

Stares at the fireplace.

Baxter stirs, raising his head... gets up.

The sound of the back door opening. His voice greeting Baxter in the kitchen. She has to collect herself.

'Hello darling, why are you sitting inside on a night like this?'

He walks past her, opening the patio doors.

I saw you. But she didn't. *I heard you.*

She goes into the bathroom, washes her face, combs her hair, tries to compose herself.

Outside, he is sitting with his legs stretched, ankles crossed, Baxter lying beside him. On the patio table are two glasses of wine.

'How was your day?'

What he always asks.

'There...' She clears her throat. '...was a power cut. I was home early.'

He lifts his glass, running his other hand along Baxter's back. 'And what were you doing all day, old son?'

He had wanted a son. She wouldn't have minded a girl or a boy.

Kim got one of each.

'What's for dinner?'

She has to think about it. 'Lasagne.' She brought it out of the freezer this morning. Seems like days... weeks ago.

'Clara, are you okay?'

I heard you.

Why can't she say it? She picks up her glass, sips from it. 'I'm fine. How was your day?' What she always asks.

He sighs. 'The planners are making us change...' She doesn't want to look at him, can't bear to as he speaks. 'They don't seem to understand this'll impact...' Maybe there'll be a clue in his face, how long he and Kim have been... weeks, months, *years*? 'Neither do they realise...' He pulls the knot of his tie, already slackened, the top button of his shirt undone, same as usual after work, just like he seems exactly the same... her eyes move down to his trouser fly, could she have been mistaken? The TV could have been on, a voice like his...

Ringing.

Her ring tone.

She takes her mobile out of her pocket.

Gazes at Kim's name on the screen.

Kim, who has always looked out for her; Kim, who she confided in; Kim, who she turned to first if she had a problem, even before Drew.

'Are you not going to answer it?' Drew stands, walks down the garden, Baxter trotting behind.

'Hello.'

'I was about to hang up! Are you in the middle of something?'

Her voice also sounding the same as usual. Drew throws a stick; Baxter runs for it.

Oh, that's so good.

'Just to say I've booked the carvery for four o'clock on Sunday, they didn't have anything earlier.'

Exactly the same, no hint of anything in her voice. Drew is laughing, making Baxter jump into the air, throwing the stick again.

'No doubt Stevie's still eating like a horse. Maybe, I should warn them he's coming!'

A pause, when Clara would usually have laughed. 'Clara?'

'Actually, I… am in the middle of something.'

'Oh, sorry. I'll let you go. Night, love.'

Drew is lying on his back on the grass, Baxter chewing the stick beside him. 'Give it to me, Bax. Give. It. To. Me.'

She goes inside the house, walking to the sideboard, picking up the photograph of Stevie and Sophie in their school uniforms. Sophie is a mirror image of Kim. Stevie doesn't take after her at all… Clara rummages in the sideboard drawers.

The album of old photographs.

Kim and Brian's wedding day.

She studies Brian's face, holds it beside Stevie's. They are both blonde, but Stevie isn't like his father either. She takes a sharp intake of breath, looking through the patio doors at her husband's fair head on the lawn. Was it going on even back then… Brian was in hospital for months after the operation; Drew helped, cutting the grass, doing odd jobs.

Then Brian was home, getting stronger; Kim was pregnant with Stevie... as the years passed it seemed the tumour wasn't coming back, and Sophie came along, but then Brian had a routine check; he didn't even make the month they gave him to live. Drew was often over there again, fixing things, whatever needed done. 'I don't know what I'd do without him.' Kim was in tears as she said it. Clara had been proud of him, how kind he'd been.

The patio door opens; Baxter pads in behind. He stops beside her. 'Wow, look at that suit. The lapels!'

She makes herself turn her head towards him, forms the words: *I know about you and Kim...*

He takes off his tie, draping it over his shoulder. 'He was a good bloke, Brian.' He puts his hand on her waist; she has to stop herself from flinching. 'Are you sure you're okay?'

His fingers tighten on her waist; she nods, and he walks away... his soft tread on the stairs... the rattle of hangers on the wardrobe rail, and she crumples, her knees just give way and she's on the floor, her hand over her mouth.

Sunday.

She almost cancelled, almost rang Kim. 'Sorry, I'm not well.' Drew thought they should cancel because she's been off colour, not herself.

But they are here, sitting in the hotel bar, waiting for them to arrive; she is waiting to see him and Kim together, to see the way they look at each other, talk to each other, to see what she must have missed seeing.

'Happy birthday, Stevie!'

Drew is on his feet, clapping him on the back.

She has to pull herself together.

Behind them Kim is smiling and apologising for being late.

Her eyes meet Kim's; she has to turn away. Turns towards Stevie, clears her throat. 'Look at the height of you. You've grown even in one term.'

'Maybe, you lot are getting smaller.'

'Stevie!' Kim admonishes.

Drew mock punches his shoulder. 'When you're his age anyone over fifty is a geriatric.'

'It's the amount he eats. He only got back from uni yesterday, and he's already emptied the fridge.'

'Don't exaggerate, Mother.'

Brian was also tall and broad-shouldered. Kim is looking at her; she has to stop staring at Stevie. Sophie sits beside her; Clara turns her head towards her. 'Hello sweetheart.'

She smiles back, unzipping the handbag on her lap.

'Off for the school holidays, then?'

She nods.

She's the quiet one, not like Stevie the attention seeker, who is asking a waiter for a type of beer he doesn't seem to have heard of.

Sophie's side profile—still all Kim. She is looking into her bag, frowning, and Clara gazes at the inhaler inside, remembering Brian had asthma, that it ran in his family.

They are both Brian's. The relief is overwhelming.

'Are you okay, Clara?'

She has to turn her head towards Kim.

'You're very pale.'

'She hasn't been well all weekend,' says Drew.

'I'm fine. So, what are you doing over the summer, Soph?'

'I got a job.'

'In Tesco,' adds Kim, as the waiter arrives with the drinks. 'She started on Friday, and luckily there's a bus…'

Friday. Clara waits for Kim to glance at Drew, for her eyes to register a sign of guilt at the mention of that day.

'Clara?' says Drew.

She realises that the waiter is beside her. 'A glass of wine, madam?'

'No… I mean, yes… thanks.'

'Clara, you really don't seem yourself,' says Kim.

'She wasn't well when I came home from work on Friday.' Drew's expression, his eyes, not a flicker of guilt either.

Everyone is looking at her. She has to say something. 'I… think I've eaten something that's disagreed with me, that's all.'

'Is that why you left work early on Friday?' asks Kim.

Clara stares at her.

'I saw you coming out. I was driving past, or rather Sal was driving. We were going shopping. She needed something to wear to the wedding, didn't I tell you her eldest's getting married?'

Clara can only stare at her.

'Anyway, it took all afternoon for her to find

something.'

But Clara heard her and Drew...

'What had you for lunch on Friday?'

Kim couldn't have seen her coming out of work...

'She usually buys sandwiches,' Drew says for her.

Kim couldn't have been shopping...

They are all looking at her. She stands quickly, spilling her drink, 'Sorry, I...' hurrying across the room.

In the Ladies, she locks herself in a cubicle. Closes the lid, sits, tries to slow her breathing.

After a while, Kim's voice at the other side of the door. 'Clara?'

She has to come out. Kim is leaning against the sinks. 'Poor love, I never trust bought sandwiches.'

Trust.

Clara gets out her phone to ring a taxi.

'I'll take you home, the car's outside.'

'No!'

Kim looks startled at her sharpness.

At home, she sits on the sofa. Tries to sort it out in her head. Kim must think she suspects that they were together on Friday, that was why she lied about being out with her friend... but then she must always be lying, she and Drew, lying to and deceiving her.

She puts a hand to her necklace, the diamond pendant Drew gave her for their twentieth anniversary, which she never takes off. Exactly what she would have picked for herself. 'That's because we're soul mates,' Drew had said. They'd laughed at how corny this sounded. 'Corny, but true,' Drew added, and that had started them off again.

Her eyes fill. She covers her face with her hands, rocking her body from side to side, breathing in gasps, sobbing so loudly she almost doesn't hear the door opening.

She stills.

But it's just Baxter. He pads across the room, puts his head on her knee. She strokes his nose... it calms her. She leans back, closing her eyes, she is so tired... how did Kim know she left work early, she couldn't have seen her as she said... she can't think straight, she is so tired, she has barely slept in days...

A noise wakens her; it's daylight, there's a blanket over her. Sounds like water running into the basin in the kitchen...

She hears him approaching, the rap of his work brogues on the wooden floor, closes her eyes again... he must be standing over her now, as the scent of his aftershave gets stronger... there's the sound of... something being set down? His footsteps walk away again... she hears him talking to Baxter, then the click of the back door closing.

She opens her eyes; steam is rising from the mug on the table next to her. A piece of toast on a plate beside it. He is always considerate, always doing the small things. 'You do realise how lucky you are.' The countless times Kim has said that.

She sips the tea; her stomach makes loud gurgling noises. She makes herself eat the toast.

Then gets her mobile out of her bag.

I know.

Repeats it out loud as she waits for her to answer.

'Hello Clara. How are you now, love?'

Her voice throws Clara, the concern in it.

'Are you feeling any... sorry, hold on a tick,' speaking in a different direction and volume, 'I'm on the phone, Stevie!' A pause, and then, '*Completely cold?*' A pause. 'It'll not do you any harm.'

'Sorry, Stevie's in the shower and it went cold on him. He's making a fuss. Will you tell Drew it's gone again?'

Clara doesn't understand what she's talking about.

'It's worked fine since he fixed it on Friday, but now we've no hot water again.'

Matter-of-fact. Does she not feel guilty at all at the mention of that day? Unless—it occurs to Clara—she has nothing to feel guilty about.

'He was at your house on Friday?'

'Yes, I texted him before I went out with Sal; he said he had a cancelled meeting, that he'd call over and look at the boiler.'

It might not have been Kim... why had she not thought of this possibility before? It was only Drew she heard. He could be having an affair with... his PA for instance; she was recently divorced, Clara remembered, and attractive, bubbly... He got the text; they were in his car...

Tears run down her cheeks, but absurdly she is smiling. It wasn't Kim. Of course not!

'And he's got your door key.' Clara wipes her tears with her fingers.

'Yes, but Soph was here anyway. I know I've said it a hundred times, I really don't know what we'd do without him.'

'But…'

A pulse beats in Clara's head.

'But Sophie was working on Friday, you said she…'

'Yes, in the morning. Her shift finishes at one.'

Clara's hand flies to her mouth.

'Oh, there's the doorbell. Sorry, Clara, have to go.'

She jumped to the wrong conclusion about Kim, Clara reminds herself, trying to calm down, now she's doing it again. Sophie mustn't have gone home after her shift. She… went to a friend's or… down the town.

The pulse continues to beat in her head.

She wasn't in the house. Drew was there with his PA. People had affairs with colleagues all the time. It happened in her own work, she knew of several… the house was empty, Drew seized the opportunity.

Sophie wasn't at home.

She couldn't have been.

She is sitting in her car.

It is parked where she can see the entrance to the supermarket, so she will see Sophie coming out. *I was passing, thought I'd give you a lift…* then somehow steer the conversation to last Friday.

She could ask Sophie did she want to go shopping this Friday, that Clara was off that day, then ask her what she did after work last week… Sophie will reply that she went down the town… there's jeans she saw… that's what a fourteen-year-old would do, spend her wages right away.

A car drives past... a black Audi.

Same as...

She recognises the registration.

It turns into a parking space.

Clara's eyes move to the registration plate again; she must have misread...

The driver's door opens.

Drew gets out.

He closes the door; leans against the side of the car.

If he turns his head, he'll see her.

But he's looking straight ahead towards the shop entrance, the same way Clara was a moment ago.

His posture alters, and Clara sees who he has just seen. Sophie is coming out of the building; she takes another step, and his hand raises, waving; she looks blank for a moment, then her face changes when she sees who it is, her step falters, and Clara can no longer breathe as she watches Sophie walk slowly towards the car, watches her getting into the passenger seat, then the car reversing back and driving away.

Clara stares after it...

Stares after it, remembering... Sophie wasn't always the quiet one... was the same as Stevie, full of beans, outgoing... changed when she was... nine, about nine, became introverted, Kim had been worried she was being bullied at school.

Clara opens the car door just in time, brings back up her breakfast.

She starts the car, drives towards Kim's; has to stop at

the side of the road; she has nothing left to bring up. Drives again... don't think, just drive... drive... how could she not have known... how is it possible... just drive, don't think... how could she not have... She turns in Kim's driveway. Stops her car beside Kim's, hurries towards the house, past the study window. She's not at her desk.

Through the back door, into the kitchen, *'Kim?'* her voice a sob. She hears a footstep. 'Oh...' she tries to compose herself, 'Where-where's your mum, Stevie?'

'Gone out.'

'B-but,' she flounders, 'her car...'

'Her friend, what's-her-name... Sal, picked her up.'

Clara tries to process this.

'You okay?'

She sits at the kitchen table. Her legs will no longer hold her up.

'She's always skiving, never does any work. You look awful, do you want a cup of tea or something?'

Clara has to gather herself. 'No, I... I have to go.'

She gets back into the car.

Takes her mobile out of her bag; bile comes up her throat as she calls him; she swallows.

It rings.

Her heart is beating louder than the ringing.

No answer.

She stares unseeing through the windscreen.

Unseeing through the windscreen.

It keeps replaying in her head, Sophie's step faltering, her face changing when she realises who it is, the distress, then resignation...

Her phone bleeps. Sorry, missed your call. At lunch with client. Any better today? Xx

She types: Where are you now?

At office. Why?

She starts the car, begins to drive... her step faltering... blank it out, concentrate on driving... her step faltering... how could they not have known, suspected... Stevie was always there, he was never alone with... then she remembers, Sophie used to swim on Mondays, Kim and Clara's yoga night, Drew took Stevie to football practice first, then he was alone in the car with...

She turns into the car park beside his office.

Sees his car.

She parks.

Somehow steadies herself.

He comes out of the building. Walks towards his car.

It startles him when she appears. '*Clara?* What on earth! Are you okay? Has something...'

'We need to talk.'

'What about? I've a site meeting with the planners, what do you want to talk about?' Clearly irritated now, although there's no panic in his eyes, but then he knows how stupid she is, to never realise, never suspect...

'It's an important meeting,' he opens the driver's door, 'I can't be late. Look, we'll talk later.'

She opens the passenger door, gets in beside him as he starts the engine.

He's even more annoyed. 'What can't wait until

tonight?'

They pull out of the car park.

'I know.'

His head turns towards her. 'Know what? What do you mean? You're not making sense.'

'Friday… I was at Kim's, on Friday.'

The air changes in the car. She can sense his panic, even though his face remains the same, staring at the road ahead.

The seatbelt reminder is bleeping and he grabs for his. 'Clara, it must be because you're not well, it's making you talk gibberish. Look, this is a very important meeting. I can't believe you came to the office.'

The car picks up speed; a nerve is jumping in his neck; his knuckles are turning white from clenching the steering wheel. Her seat belt reminder gets louder, more insistent. 'Put on your belt!'

'Sophie.'

As she says her name something unravels inside Clara, something she hadn't realised she'd been keeping together, and then she is screaming and striking out, hitting his shoulder, his head. He tries to fend her off…

A thump, and the car tilts, and then it pauses, or so it seems to Clara, before it starts to roll, and she sees the wall, just before…

She knows it is him in the room with her. Sandalwood, his aftershave, that she buys him each Christmas.

The sound of the door opening, footsteps… a doctor, the one with the squeaky shoes.

Drew begins talking when the door opens. 'It's a beautiful card, Clara, everyone at your office sending their best wishes, darling...'

One of her eyelids is lifted, then the other. He's gentler than the other doctors. The rustle of paper. Clara pictures pages on a clipboard being flicked through, then there's the faint creak of the door opening again, clicking closed.

He sighs loudly, and then must move closer, his face must be above hers because she can feel his breath on her forehead, and she tries to channel all of her will, to direct it to her eyes, to open, to see the shock on his face, channelling everything she has for them to open, for the eyelids to lift...

It doesn't work. Never works.

She tries to calm herself; Kim will be here soon, the whiff of nicotine from her clothes, she hasn't smoked since she was a teenager, the balm of her voice. 'Hello Clara, love, how are you today?' The touch of her lips on Clara's cheek, her hand enclosing hers. 'I passed your doctor in the corridor,' she said last time, 'you have to waken up, if just to see him. Movie star, that's all I'm going to say. You'll have to see for yourself.' Her hand pressed as she kept talking. 'We all miss you so much, we can't wait until you're better,' her voice cracked, 'pl-please waken up, sweetheart.'

She'll be here soon; Clara tells herself again. Think only of that.

His face is still above hers. *No one will believe you,* what he said, his breath like now against her skin. Another time: *She likes it. She'll deny it as well.*

The sound of the door opening; something touches her head, his hand? He strokes her hair; a ripple of revulsion passes through her.

'Hello Clara, love. I've brought someone to see you.'

The scent of apple blossom.

'Hello Auntie Clara.'

Sophie's beautiful, hesitant voice.

'Talk to Auntie Clara, Soph.'

'Stevie... Stevie's coming to see you tomorrow. You... you're only allowed two visitors.'

'Tell her about yesterday, about the lady in Tesco,' prompts Kim.

'This... this lady had a bag of tomatoes, and... they fell out onto the floor and... can she hear me?'

'Yes, of course she can!' Kim's sharp voice, unlike her.

'Soph, what Mum means is we're all hoping she can... Why don't you go and get yourself some hot chocolate... Here, there's the money.'

The sound of the door opening, then closing.

'I know she can. She's my sister. I know she can!'

'C'mon Kim, you've been so strong.'

'I... it's just...' her voice breaking.

The rustle of material; Clara tries to block out the image of his arm around her, rubbing her back.

'Kim, we're going to have to face up to the possibility that she might not... we need to prepare ourselves.'

'What do you mean?'

'I talked to one of the doctors this morning... about the life support.'

'But...' Clara pictures Kim blankly staring at him. '*They* can't decide! It's up to us.'

'To me as her next of kin.'

'No!'

'I can't bear it either, Kim, but we're only prolonging...'

'She's going to wake up!'

The door creaks... 'It's okay, Soph. Mum's okay.'

Kim's hand on hers, holding it tightly, the sound of her crying.

'I think I should take Sophie home.'

No! Clara silently screams.

'You and Clara can spend some time together, just the two of you. I'll take Soph...'

No! Clara's heart is ripping apart.

Kim lifts up her hand, kissing it, then holds it against her cheek, sobbing. You can do this, Clara tells herself. She can, if she tries hard enough, she wants to so much, to press Kim's hand in hers... she can do this.

'Clara... Clara, love, please... you have to... *Please* waken up.'

Clara tries to channel her desperation, pictures it flowing from her heart, along the blood vessels, flowing towards her hand, gaining force, gaining momentum...

'Okay Soph, I'll take you home now.'

All of her love for Kim, for Sophie, for Stevie, flowing to her fingers, to press Kim's, to press, rushing from her heart, from every part of her, all going to her fingers, to press, for Sophie, for Sophie...

Shouting.

The sound of the door opening.

Joyous shouting.

Kim shouting for a doctor.

Crush

I try not to think about Valerie now. I can manage it for a while, but then she'll catch me unawares, slipping into my head when I'm thinking about something else, pushing other thoughts out.

'You've got a crush on my wife, that's all,' her husband said. 'When you're older you'll look back and laugh about it. Believe me.'

Once, I went for a whole week without thinking about her, but *The Rolling Stones* came on the radio, and I dreamt about her that night, about the day I first went to her house.

The stereo was up so loud she mustn't have heard the doorbell. I rang it again. '*Because I used to love her, but it's all over now*,' belted out of an open window.

She was dancing around the room with a yellow duster in her hand. She bobbed her head, wiggling her bum, holding the duster to her mouth like a microphone, twirling.

'Oh!'

She stood still, looking warily at what she could see of me, just my eyes and forehead above the windowsill.

'I'm Dean!' I shouted above the music. 'I'm here to do the garden!'

'Oh,' she said again.

She introduced herself when she came outside. 'I'm Valerie Rourke,' she said, holding out her hand and smiling. 'Well, I'm sure you can see why we need your help out here.'

She gazed beyond me across the large garden.

'Yeah…' I couldn't take my eyes away from her face. 'I mean it's not that bad.'

She showed me around, and we arranged that I would do two afternoons a week.

I was cutting the lawn on my first day when she appeared at the back door of the house, mouthing through the noise of the mower, 'Cup of tea?'

I stood awkwardly on the step, not wanting to tread dirt onto her kitchen floor.

'Take off your boots if you like.'

She put biscuits onto a plate, indicating for me to sit at the table. My big toe was showing through a hole in my sock. I crossed my ankles below the chair, my face growing hot.

'So, how long have you been gardening, Dean?' she asked, as we drank tea from china mugs.

I almost replied, *Since I left school*, but stopped myself in time.

'Bout two years.'

She nodded. 'Do you live with your parents?'

'With me ma.'

I looked away, my face on fire. I was eighteen and still living with my mother. I couldn't afford a place of my own, and anyway, Ma would be lonely by herself. I could feel Mrs Rourke's eyes on me. I stared straight ahead, at the huge cooker against the wall opposite. The whole downstairs of our house would fit easily into this kitchen.

I stood. 'Ta for the tea, Mrs Rourke.'

'Call me Valerie,' she said, smiling.

Her husband was always at work when I was there. She mentioned him sometimes; 'Adam wants that shrub cut back,' or, 'Don't ask me what's wrong with the lawnmower, that's Adam's department.' Then one day she said, 'Adam's away on business. Do you want to come over later?'

We sat in the room in which I had watched her dancing that first day. She brought us wine, sitting at the other end of the sofa. She crossed her legs, smoothing her skirt. The toenails of her bare feet were painted pink. Her hand rested on the cushion between us; I imagined casually reaching over and taking hold of it.

I almost kissed her that night. We were at the door. She peeked outside. 'Just in case.' She giggled.

'Jus in case what?' The wine gave me courage. 'Someone sees us together?'

She laughed. 'Now, now, Deany boy. I'm old enough to be your mother.'

'I don fancy me ma.'

She laughed louder, pushing me out and closing the door. I could still hear her laughter as I walked away.

Our tea break at four o'clock became a routine. She wanted to know about the other gardens I did, what the people were like.

'Mondays, I do Wes Hixon's. His garden's ace. There's a massive pond, couldn believe it when I first seen the size of the water lilies.'

'Oh yes W-W-Wes,' she said. 'With the fr-fr-frightful stammer.'

'Then, Tuesdays I'm at Mrs McKeel's.' I grinned,

remembering. 'Last week, she got herself locked in the bathroom when she were havin a shower. I'd to fetch a ladder, climb in through the window.'

'Was she naked?'

'Well… well, she… she'd a towel.'

'Who's stammering now.' Valerie laughed. Her laughter faded and she leaned forward, looking intently at me, her voice husky, 'Bet she was *really* pleased to see you.' Her eyes held mine. She felt the same way I did! I reached my hand towards her, to touch her face, my heart thudding in my ears. She gazed past me, drawing back, 'Adam…'

I looked behind me, at the man standing in the doorway.

'Adam,' she said again. 'This… is Dean. The gardener.'

He stepped forward, holding out his hand to me. 'I'm the husband,' smirking, as if he'd said something clever.

He wasn't how I had imagined him. I had pictured him as tall and good looking—someone impressive; someone who would impress Valerie. But he was small and overweight with wispy, greying hair.

I glanced at Valerie, who was watching her husband, eyes nervous. In fact, it was more than that. She seemed afraid. He was a bully, I realised. It was the ones you least expected, like Da he didn't look threatening. Ma never mentioned it, not even now he was gone. Sometimes I think I dreamt it, the thuds and muffled shouting from downstairs, that I could still hear even with my head under the covers.

I shook Adam's soft hand firmly in my work-hardened one.

'You're doing a great job in the garden,' he said.

I muttered something about getting back to it, and he followed me outside.

He watched me pulling out weeds. 'You like working here, then?' he asked.

I nodded, not looking at him.

'Yes, well, it's hard not to get on with Val. She's such a sociable person. We had a young man helped us out before with the garden. He'd have been about your age. He was greatly taken with Val, and of course she flirted with him. She's such a terrible flirt, wanting everyone to fall in love with her.'

I kept my head down, yanking out another weed.

'"You've got a crush on my wife, that's all," I told him. "When you're older you'll look back and laugh about it. Believe me."'

My time with Valerie wasn't the same after that. She was on edge when I was in the kitchen in case he appeared, wanting me outside again as quickly as possible.

'Are you finished?' She reached for my half-full mug of tea.

I put my hand on her arm. 'Leave him.'

She stared at me as though I'd gone mad. Then, understanding dawned in her eyes, and she laughed. 'What, and go and live with you and your mother?'

'I *know*,' I said.

'What are you talking about?'

'I know you're feared of him.'

She laughed again, pulling her arm free from my grasp. 'Deany boy has got a vivid imagination.'

'Don call me that.'

'But you are just a boy.' She ruffled my hair.

I pulled her against me. She didn't kiss me back. I let her go, and she stumbled away. There was blood on her lip; I hadn't meant to hurt her! She gazed silently at me; I tried to find the right words, to beg her not to let it ruin everything. But then she opened her arms, beckoning me into them.

I went back to the house after dark, scarcely able to breathe with anticipation, but he was there, his voice loud though the open window.

'You really expect me to believe that?'

Valerie didn't reply, or if she did I didn't hear her.

'You *really* expect me to believe that you tripped and hit your lip on the door?'

There was a chink, like of a bottle touching glass, and I remembered our evening together, how she'd smiled at me as she poured us more wine.

'Did you and the gardener have a lover's tiff?'

'Don't be ridiculous.'

'Is your life really *so* boring, Val, that you need a thrill out of leading him on? I thought you'd learned your lesson last time.'

'Dean likes me, that's all. I haven't done anything to encourage him.'

He laughed. It was loud and ugly, and she shouted at him to shut up. But he kept on, and she said something else, but I couldn't make it out because of his laughter.

There was a silence, and I knew what that meant. Da would be still and silent watching TV, but he was angry, I could see it in his eyes, and I'd slip out of the room and upstairs before it started, willing myself to fall asleep so I didn't hear.

There was the sharp ring of breaking glass.

I ran down the side of Valerie's house. The back door wasn't locked.

He had hold of her. There was blood on her arm, her hands. She screamed when she saw me. How many times had I heard it starting downstairs and buried my head under the covers? It was either Ma or me. How could I have been such a coward?

Valerie shouted, '*What are you doing here?*'

He walked towards me, opening his mouth to speak; there was blood, *her* blood on his hands.

My fist caught him off balance.

He stumbled backwards, towards the fireplace… his foot caught on the rug, and then, as if in slow motion, he was falling…

The back of his head hit the hearth.

Valerie wouldn't look at me at the trial. 'He seemed to have a crush on me,' she said, when they asked about our relationship. She denied that she was fighting with her husband that night. 'I broke my wine glass, that was all. It cut my hand.' She sobbed. 'He wouldn't hit me. He has never hurt me.'

My lawyer didn't tell the truth either. He said that Valerie abused her position as my employer, that I was like a toy to her, that she had used me to make her husband jealous. He said it was obvious I was also a victim, and the only just verdict would be accidental death.

The jury didn't agree with him though; they decided it was manslaughter.

Afterwards, I wrote to Valerie, asking her to visit me.

I used to send her letters every week, but I've stopped writing to her now. I try not to think about her, but I can't get her voice out of my head, what she whispered as she held me in her arms after I kissed her, *'You're right, I am frightened of him… He's out tonight… It'll just be you and me Deany boy.'*

I wonder who is looking after her garden; who is taking care of all my gardens.

It's what I think about, when I can push Valerie out of my mind—the sun on my back, soil running through my fingers, and the smell of newly-mown grass.

The Good Neighbour

He's the cocky type, striding along the pavement, whistling because he's so pleased with himself. He doesn't look at me when we pass, a woman over sixty, not so much as a glance, as though I don't exist.

But he should notice me, he should stop and say, *Hi, I'm Keith. I've moved into number 31.* Then I'll reply, *Welcome to the street, Keith! I'm Barbara, from number 22. If there's anything you need just pop round!* He'll have already heard about me from the curtain twitchers, no doubt they've noticed I go out earlier in the mornings now, at the same time Keith is swaggering his way to work.

He's heading towards Barclays, on the corner of Mill Street. He could have told me about his job, if he'd stopped for a chat. A cashier, he'd have had to admit. He doesn't carry a briefcase, so he must just be on the desk. Not a lot to be proud about then, but he does it so well. His suit is too well cut, too expensive for just a cashier, so he must have ambitions, aspirations. But then he's young, not the wrong side of sixty.

When he remembers his manners one of these days and speaks to me, I'll bake him a welcoming gift. He'll have heard I like to do this when the neighbours were gossiping about me.

He'll ask me in, and put the kettle on. *Oh, these are something else, Barbara,* he'll say, after tasting my scones. *To die for?* I'll ask, and he'll smile, *Absolutely.* Then a frown will wrinkle his smooth brow as he remembers what the twitchers said, but they were exaggerating, must have been. Look at her, just a harmless old biddy in her elasticated skirt, lace-up shoes, and twinkling smile. *Dangerous*—that was the word number 25 used, but there must be history between those two.

He doesn't remember his manners though, doesn't pause for a chat, and I wonder if I'm judging him harshly; the swagger might be a front for shyness, so I make the first move on the pavement.

'Good morning!'

He keeps on walking, as if I haven't spoken.

'Excuse me?'

He stops, turns his head.

'I'm Barbara. From number 22.'

He looks blankly at me.

'It's Keith, isn't it?'

'How do you know my name?'

'Oh… one of the neighbours mentioned it.'

His gaze moves to the houses along the street. 'I don't know no one here.'

He will have to improve his grammar if he is going to climb the banking ranks.

I smile. 'You know me now.'

His eyes drop down my blouse and skirt, socks and shoes. 'Yeah.' He sniggers, walking on.

Why does he have to be rude like that? Although… perhaps, I should make allowances. It wasn't a good time to chat; he didn't want to be late for work, not when he's trying to get a promotion.

But he'll be knocking on my door tonight. He will have thought better of his snigger. We can watch *Corrie* together. He never misses it. He'll have got changed into old jogging bottoms and a faded t-shirt, like he does every night to watch the telly.

Thumping on the door. I smooth my skirt, and put on lipstick. All right, all right, no need to break it down.

'Keith, what a lovely surprise!'

His tie is loosened, and he has undone the top button of his shirt. He needs a shower, but I don't mind, I like the sweet-sour smell of male sweat.

He shoves the bag in his hands at me; it bursts open, and a couple of scones fall out, hitting the floor, crumbs everywhere.

'Come in,' I smile. Not everyone likes scones, I should have thought of that. Or he could have a wheat allergy.

'Don't come snooping round mine again! You hear?'

Leaving a bag of scones on his windowsill is hardly *snooping*, I would know after all as a retired police officer. Maybe, I should advise him to start closing his curtains at night, you never know who is about, especially with him working in the bank. Anyone could be outside, watching.

'I know your type.' He points his finger at me. 'The local effing busybody. Poking your nose in ev'rything.'

The twitchers must have got to him. *Busybody.* That'll be from number 27—*Watch out for Barbara, Keith, don't let her get in on you,* leaning on her walking frame, like she'd fall without it. Which she didn't, when I took it away for her own good; it was just a prop, a habit. Her son came to my door, accusing me of abusing his mother. He actually said, 'Stay away from her, or I'll call the police.'

Anyway, it's very rude of Keith, to point at me like that. I give a neighbour a bag of scones, and that's the thanks I get. He'll think that I won't be out the next day, passing him on his way to work.

'Good morning!'

He doesn't acknowledge me, keeps whistling on.

'Do you like working at Barclays?' I call after him.

He stops, turns slowly around.

'No briefcase, I see?'

He's deciding what to do, now he knows I've been following him. There's anger in his eyes, and I glance at the house windows to my right, then left—*witnesses*, Keith.

But then he laughs, as if realising something is funny.

'See you tonight,' I call to him as he walks on.

Afterwards I get my hair done. I want to look nice when Keith comes over later. And I buy some new flour.

He knocks on the door this time, no thumping like last time, and I almost open it wide, before changing my mind, and putting the chain on.

He smiles through the gap between the door and the frame. 'Ev'ning Barbara.' Again, he hasn't got changed out of his suit, just his tie is slackened. 'Thanks for the cake.'

'Wheat-free,' I reply.

'How did you get in, Barbara?' The smile seems to have set on his face. 'It's just I'm curious, that's all,' he goes on, and I almost take off the chain and open the door. But he's come straight over, hasn't changed into his scruffy jogging bottoms and old t-shirt. He hasn't come to watch *Corrie* with me. 'How did you get in?' he repeats.

When I don't respond his eyes narrow, glancing at the security chain; I can almost hear the galloping of his brain—*I could force the door, warn her off properly…* but now he's smiling again, as if his face has remembered it's meant to be. 'See you tomorrow, Barbara.'

But I don't go out the next morning to see him off to work, I wouldn't want him to think me predictable. I'm a twitcher for a change, making sure he has left his house, giving him a little wave from behind the curtain; he doesn't slow or turn his head as he goes past, but I know he'll be thinking about me, wondering where I am.

He is keeping number 31 clean and tidy, which is surprising for a man on his own. Even the cushions on the sofa are plumped and carefully arranged. My cake is no longer on his kitchen bench, where I left it yesterday. I find it in the bin. He mustn't have a sweet tooth.

Upstairs, the bathroom is spic and span as well. I squirt some of his aftershave onto my wrist, breathing him in. He has repainted the room blue. It was yellow. They had been appreciative at first, the new people in 31, the ones before Keith, asking me over for dinner to say thanks for the tutoring, it was so good of me to spare the time to help their youngest, but then one of the twitchers told them I wasn't a retired teacher.

His bedroom is the only untidy room in the house. He hasn't made the bed; the sheets are tangled, the duvet trailing on the floor.

I have a bath when I get home, and put on a new blouse, but he doesn't come over after work. I don't see him until the following day.

'Morning, Barbara.' He turns around as he says it, walking beside me, in the wrong direction to Barclays.

'You'll be late for work.'

'Were you ever in the army, Barbara?'

'The *army*? No, actually…'

'The way you made my bed, I'd call that military precision.'

He puts his hand on my shoulder. 'I could get used to a woman's touch about the place.'

I reach up to keep his hand there, but he has already turned, walking the other way again.

It stays with me—the feel of his fingers, the tingling sensation spreading from my shoulder. Stays with me as I let myself in. Stays with me as I make the bed. Stays with me as I take the aftershave from the bathroom cabinet.

His face appears behind me in the mirror; the bottle slips from my grasp, clattering into the sink, but he's smiling, his hand on my arm, guiding me out of the bathroom. Guiding me down the stairs.

'Give me the key, Barbara.'

I sit on the sofa, patting it, for him to sit beside me.

He sighs heavily, before remembering he's being friendly, because that is obviously the plan.

'The key,' he says again, once he's sat down.

I reach over and take his hand, putting it on my thigh.

Disgust. He can't hide it. His hand recoils, as if bitten. He probably meant to sugar me up a bit to get the key back, but his hand on my decrepit thigh is too much, and it takes him a moment to regain composure.

I try again, to place his hand, smiling at him—it won't be so bad.

This time his eyes narrow, his breathing audible, and then he is shouting and lashing out, and I know what will happen as a result.

He'll lose his job in Barclays, although he was never going to get to the briefcase stage anyway, he doesn't have it in him. But they can't employ someone even as a cashier who attacks a sad old biddy.

Maybe, the next new people at number 31 will be good types. They'll know to speak to Barbara at number 22, to appreciate her scones, to ask her over, to let her be a good neighbour.

Shame about Keith, although he's come to his senses now, drawing back; his hands are shaking, in fact he seems to be trembling all over.

He stares at me, slumped on the sofa, backing against the wall at the other side of the room, as if *I* am the attacker.

I put a hand up to my face; it is starting to swell already, around my eye.

He shakes his head, 'I… I didn't… mean to…'

My lip is wet. I hold out my hand, showing him my red fingers. He gazes at them with horror and panic in his eyes; I can almost hear the whirring of his brain— *She'll go to the police. I'll lose my job! I'll have a criminal record!*

His shoulders sag, and his head goes down under the weight of these thoughts.

Poor Keith has lost his swagger.

'You could...'

His head shoots up.

'...make it up to me.'

I look away from him, in case the disgust has returned, and when I turn my face towards him again, he seems resigned.

'J-just,' he struggles to speak, 'one-once.'

I smile at him.

He tries to pull back his lips in return.

It's more a grimace than a smile.

'*Once*,' he repeats, as if it is up to him to decide.

Poor Keith, he's not really in a position to negotiate.

I keep on smiling

Rosemary Mairs lives in County Antrim, Northern Ireland. She studied Psychology at Queen's University Belfast. Her stories have been published in anthologies and won prizes including The Writers' Bureau Short Story Competition. 'My Father's Hands' received The Society of Authors' Tom-Gallon Trust Award. The semi-autobiographical 'A Beginner's Guide to Stammering' was longlisted for the 2018 Bristol Prize. 'A Recycled Marriage' was a 2020 Eludia Award Finalist.